Mrs. Fuller

Crown-Harden

Volume 2

Mrs. Fuller

Crown-Harden
Volume 2

ISBN/EAN: 9783337272661

Printed in Europe, USA, Canada, Australia, Japan

Cover: Foto ©Andreas Hilbeck / pixelio.de

More available books at **www.hansebooks.com**

CROWN-HARD

BY

MRS. FULLER.

" Crystal bubbles
Charm us at once away from all our troubles."

IN THREE VOLUMES.

VOL. II.

LONDON:
HURST AND BLACKETT, PUBLISHERS,
13, GREAT MARLBOROUGH STREET.
1873.

CROWN-HARDEN.

CHAPTER I.

GREY above, and silken grey below. Is all this sky? A flash of sunlight pierces the mist, and a glare of white rises to meet it from below.

Now you begin to see that there is a boundless circle of water all around, it is the green Atlantic—the fog of morning still is resting in heavy curls, like steam over its breast; but what fiendish monsters are these, taking advantage of the absence of man to disport themselves in such a graceless manner? great, black, shining monsters of the deep. One leaps some feet clear out of the water, and down he goes again, with a plash that would have almost shipwrecked one of the Thames model yachts; now another is up, and there go two together, so through the day these shy porpoises hold their watery orgies.

The mist has gone, and the great ocean is blue and soft as the haze that tints off the sharpness of the horizon. The hours drag on, only one little sail has passed that way all day long; as it appeared in the distance its sails flapped weakly and listlessly, till a little gentle wind came, and it is gone and leaves the great wide flood to its loneliness again.

Old sailors, as they look at the sky, say there will be wind to-night, for the sun has dipped into the ocean with an angry flush, and mare's-tail clouds are in the sky. Even now a cold wind comes up from the south-east, and blows in uncertain gusts. It darkens rapidly—the sky just now so un-broken, is a mass of hurrying clouds, that look as if something was going wrong; all is black, the wind and sea rush like a great water-fall, the waves seem broken into flinty mountains, the white horses just dimly discernible are rolling their crested manes—so it lasts throughout the night.

Morning breaks. What a change! The soft indigo of yesterday's ocean—the fierce, crashing Babel of to-day. Very grand, certainly, but what do those poor sailors think of it on board those tossing vessels that are scudding northwards?

They have soon disappeared; but what is this? A new thing has come upon the stage. By the white sails and cut of her jib she appears to be a yacht; her sails are close-reefed, she nears us rapidly—a yacht she proves to be, the most rakish little schooner that ever graced the Solent. The narrow boards of the deck are polished like a drawing-room table, but she seems in a terrible way; every third sea dashes all over her, and then swills off the decks with a gush again; her rigging bears marks of very rough treatment—the crew have been up all night working at the pumps, she sails heavy, rolls terribly, and seems to sit deep; no wonder, considering the depth of water that is sloshing about in her hold. .

But surely we recognise an old acquaintance in this poor little tangled, ill-used mermaid. Yes; it is the dainty *Ariel* that has been buffeted so unceremoniously by the rough waves. Can she ever reach the land?

But we must leave her in her difficulty, and go back a few weeks to retrace the course of the little schooner who left the English shores in such gay trim, and of her master, whom we last saw when he parted from Cecil a short way from Berkley Street.

CHAPTER II.

VILLEROY might perhaps have been inclined to postpone his expedition, but he knew that one or two of his friends had refused tempting invitations in order to fulfil their engagement with him, which had been formed some months before. Therefore, he felt bound by the arrangements that had been made, and they started from Southampton on the day originally fixed.

They were to go as far as Alexandria, which they reached after a pleasant and prosperous voyage. They rode on camels, and basked in the sun, fearless of ophthalmia; but Villeroy had been there before, and the *embonpoint* and black eyes of the Levantine belles had no charms for him, therefore he was not sorry when they put to sea again, turning the bows of the *Ariel* westward.

At Leghorn they stopped a week, when Villeroy, with his friend Spencer Carr, ran on to Florence, leaving the others at Leghorn, where his captain had many friends.

Villeroy liked Florence. Its stern, massive, dark, baronial palaces within the city, in contrast with the gay, gilded, laughing landscape without, and the Arno winding its silvery tracery around the plains, all tinted with rose-coloured almond blossom and transparent violet haze, were ever renewed pleasures to him.

He liked, too, the simple, honest Tuscan people, and received from his old friend and courier, 'Maso Santi, a huge basket of grapes, with four bouquets of early Spring flowers stuck among them, that would have warmed up even the Academy Exhibition, if the rich tints of the blossoms and the dewy gold of the grapes could have been accurately copied. There the fields were already bright with the blue and scarlet anemonies, and the pure, marble-white narcissus that grow so abundantly on those sunny slopes.

But the gallant captain, John Warden, deserves a more special notice. He was one of thirteen, the son of a father whose family was far more extensive than his fortune. John Warden, whose appetite was exceedingly good, observed that it often outran his discretion at the frugal paternal board, and therefore started off at fifteen to make a fortune in the merchant service. Though he was a very worthy fellow, he had not the peculiar art—the art of making money; and at thirty-five, finding himself no richer than at fifteen, he gladly accepted Villeroy's offer to join him in the *Ariel*, acting as his commodore.

He was a favourite with everyone—a

good-looking, broad-shouldered man, with a cheerful face, bright eyes, but, above all, a pair of long, dark brown, glossy whiskers, so that he was known by all Villeroy's friends as the "Captain with the whiskers," and was generally accosted with that popular air, whether sung or whistled. He was a modest as well as a brave man, but if any little shred of vanity did hang about him, it was on account of these well-cared-for whiskers of his; the more they chaffed him on the subject, the more inwardly persuaded he was that they would everyone of them be very proud to possess them.

Captain Warden was an Irishman too, and could sing both comic and pathetic songs, in a rich, powerful voice, that sounded very well as they sailed along the blue Mediterranean, especially when it was calm, and the soft, luscious air of the south gently filled the white sails of the *Ariel*.

But on their return, the skies were often unpropitious; the weather was squally and uncertain, assuming all the caprices, not of a gay coquette, but of a scolding woman, for it stormed much oftener than it smiled. It became so rough that Villeroy, impatient though he was to get home, put in for a week at Cadiz for some necessary repairs; and there it was that he met with a little adventure.

He, and all his friends, accepted an invitation to a ball given by one of the merchants of the place. Villeroy, like a true . Englishman, never would allow that any women were as pretty as his own countrywomen; but here he met with one who was, he was compelled to admit, unexceptionally so.

Her father was an Irishman, her mother was a Spaniard, and she herself was the young widow of a Portuguese merchant, who, enslaved by her charms, had left her the whole of his fortune, so that she was rich as well as handsome,

Doña Matilda, as she was called, had a

soft, creamy-white complexion, regular features, and a pair of deep violet-blue eyes,
that by candle-light looked darker than
black ones; though in honour of these she
was deemed a blonde, her hair and whole
appearance contradicted the appellation.

If Villeroy ever could be accused of flirt-
ing, he did so perhaps with this pretty
widow, who was clever, as well as beautiful;
for she not only possessed advantages, but
had the wit to make the greatest possible
use of them.

Her adorers comprised nearly every unmarried man of the place—indeed homage
seemed her birthright. As she danced, it
was according to her mood, sometimes with
a graceful languor, sometimes with the fire
and spirit of the Andalusian and the moun-
taineer, but either became her.

Then she threw herself down on the low-
cushioned seat near, and vowed she was
tired, using her fan with true Spanish skill.
All encircled her, entreating her to sing,

and the guitar was brought. No, she would not—she could not; and then she pouted, and pushed it away, like a naughty child.

"Ah!" they said, "if the Milor and the Señor Capitan would ask her, then, no doubt, she would not refuse them," and she swept a wicked dazzling glance at them. The prayer was made, and it was granted. She took the guitar and sang a pretty Spanish Bolero charmingly, and with as much archness as was consistent with perfect modesty—then another, and then with a dear, little foreign accent, and much expression, one of Moore's songs, shooting out a mischievous glitter from under her thick black lashes at the devoted Englishmen, whom it was clear she intended to make her prey.

After receiving so much hospitality, Villeroy could do no less than return the compliment by a dance on board the *Ariel*. The invitations were given and accepted

for the following night, as it was settled
that he should sail by daybreak the next
morning, and Doña Matilda, of course,
consented to become again the belle of the
night.

They were to dance on the polished deck
of the schooner, a beautiful supper was
laid out in the state cabin, and a band of
musicians played their softest melodies as
the boats came alongside discharging their
cargoes of beauty and gay dresses.

The round, full moon mirrored herself
in a sea as serene as the sky wherein she
floated, the pure moonlight made all as
clear as day; the tall masts, the slender
spars, the yards and ropes of the graceful
Ariel seemed traced in black with a delicate
pencil against the crystal, azure sky.

No wonder that Doña Matilda, as she
was gallantly received on the deck, looked
around her with a deep sigh of delight.

She was even more irresistible this night
than the last. Villeroy had spoken with

admiration of the genuine Spanish costume,
therefore she now wore it; the rich
black silk dress and black lace man-
tilla giving her a dignity and picturesque
grace that were really fascinating.

But the waltz, and galop, and confitures,
and iced punch recalled her thoughts to
lighter joys in a very agreeable manner.
The guests said the fête was enchanting,
and there was not a single blemish to mar
its perfection, but even such fêtes as these
must come to an end, and as the last boat
left the *Ariel*, Villeroy stood at the stern
listening to the quiet plash of the oars,
and watching the dark speck gradually disappear from sight.

The *Ariel* was now rocking to and fro, like
the cradle when the nurse gets a little impatient that her charge will not go to sleep,
and Captain Warden came up to Villeroy.

" Well, Sir, I fancy the people here are
right. I suspect we are going to have
some dirty weather. Your two friends who

left you to-night will escape a little rough treatment."

"I wished them to do so," said Villeroy, who had dropped two of his party at Leghorn, and one at Genoa. Spencer Carr had refused to part with him, but had received a letter from his mother, who was at some baths in the Pyrenees, saying she was very unwell, and he had set off for Bagnères, so that Villeroy was now alone.

"We shan't go home such a cheerful party as we came out," said the gallant captain, and sighed.

This was so unusual a phenomenon that Villeroy turned suddenly upon him, and looking in his face, saw in it an evident trouble.

"What! do you anticipate something worse than the *Ariel* can weather?" inquired Villeroy.

"I think we shall try her mettle," rejoined Captain Warden. "But, Sir, it strikes me that Doña Matilda might have had the civility to wish us farewell."

Villeroy smiled.

" She has had all the amusement out of us she can, I suppose," he replied.

" I should not have thought her a heartless lady," remarked Captain Warden. " But won't you turn in, Sir?"

" No," said Villeroy, " I am not sleepy, I shall stay up—will not you ?"

" No, thank you, Sir, I prefer remaining up, I'll just go down and have a glass of wine."

And down he dived to his cabin. Villeroy also went down to make his morning toilette, and to rest for half an hour or so on the sofa.

CHAPTER III.

WHEN Villeroy returned on deck, he found that they were already far out at sea, but the aspect of things was threatening. The sun was above the horizon, but still crimson as a red-hot cannon ball, and though there was no apparent fog, seemed gradually withdrawing himself within the thickening air. The sea was like a dark sheet of lead, above its verge some faint streaks of pale orange and livid grey were slowly dying out, and though there were no waves, there was a dull heavy swell on the ocean, as if it were labouring before a struggle. Captain Warden came up to Villeroy.

" We shall have it before long, I expect, Sir. There's a southerly gale blowing up, but I think we can still make the land. Why should not you go ashore, Sir ? You might safely entrust the *Ariel* to me."

"*I* run away from my little *Ariel?* Don't think of such a thing, Captain Warden. We shall do well enough, I have not a doubt."

" I hope so, Sir ; but this is not a good time for the Bay of Biscay."

The hours wore on, and there was not much change, except that the sky grew darker and the roll heavier.

But now, a new and disagreeable symptom made itself observed. Without much wind, there was a strange noise of whistling and moaning among the rigging and shrouds of the schooner, which gradually became louder, mingling, as the sailors fancied, with other sounds.

Towards evening, as it became dusk,

Captain Warden again approached Villeroy looking very grave.

"I don't like that noise aloft there, Sir."

"I have heard it sometimes, when the wind is shifting and veering about," said Villeroy.

"Very true, Sir. So have I. The sailors are a little superstitious about it, Sir; and they've got an odd notion in their heads. They fancy there are other sounds to be heard—a wailing—a sort of human wailing."

"Pooh! nonsense!" said Villeroy, "unless they're cowards, and are wailing themselves."

"No, Sir, not they; but they fancy the ship's doomed—that is to say—haunted."

"Idiots!" exclaimed Villeroy, "I dare say it's the boy—it's Jacob playing his silly tricks."

"No, Sir, Jacob is more frightened

than any of them. Then you, Sir, have
not heard anything ?"

" Only the row up there," said Villeroy.

" Will you take a turn or two with
me ?" asked Captain Warden.

Villeroy complied, and after taking one
or two turns stopped short, listening.
There was, he could not deny, a sound so
very like a sobbing wail, that he hardly
knew what to think. He listened intently
a minute, then walked on and the plaintive
tone seemed to die away.

" Now, Sir, what do you think ?" asked
Captain Warden.

" Certainly that it is not superhuman,
perhaps we've got the Davenport Brothers
on board."

Captain Warden smiled, but an un-
satisfied smile.

" It is curious, Sir, do not you think so ?"

" Surely *you* are not superstitious, Captain Warden ?" asked Villeroy.

" I ? Oh, no ! certainly not. But it is a

singular fact, Sir. My brother was on board the *Amelia*—she was wrecked you know, Sir, and only he and two others saved; he told me himself that all the day before he heard a sort of wailing in his ears, and so did others."

" They no doubt fancied so," said Villeroy, " but take my word for it, this is no omen or anything of the kind—winds and draughts do make the most singular sounds !"

" And you really do believe that these proceed from winds and draughts ?" asked Captain Warden incredulously.

Villeroy was doubting what answer to make, when Captain Warden gave a violent start and touched his arm.

Villeroy looked round, quite as astonished as Captain Warden could be—a black figure was gliding towards them through the gloom, veiled from head to foot. Both stared in silence, until Villeroy exclaimed :—

" Confound it ! Why it is Doña Matilda !"

And Doña Matilda it was, weeping abundantly. She commenced talking so rapidly and vehemently, that Villeroy at first could not make out her meaning. She spoke of treachery, of being betrayed, in violent reproach of he could not understand whom.

" Whom is she angry with ?" inquired Villeroy of Captain Warden in a hundred perplexities.

" Only with the ship, I think," answered Captain Warden, and so it proved to be.

According to the story of Doña Matilda, quite exhausted with her dissipation, and her two night's dancing, she had retired to a quiet corner, drawn her black velvet mantle around her, and throwing a light piece of bunting over her had fallen fast asleep : rocked by the soothing motion of the yacht, she declared she had never awoke until it was wide, broad daylight.

Then she was so alarmed, confused, and shocked at her strange situation, that she had not dared to display herself. The threatening weather, her helpless situation, a touch of sea-sickness, and the dread of the strange opinion people might form, combined with a host of nameless terrors, had taken entire possession of her, and she had been weeping and bewailing herself the last two hours—perhaps privately hoping that she would be discovered, and spared the indignity of having to produce herself; but now, in addition to other miseries, she was, as she acknowledged, most distressingly hungry.

As soon as Villeroy understood the whole case, exerting all the self-command he was master of to conceal his extreme vexation, he kindly and politely made over to her use his own cabin, hospitably desirous to make her feel as comfortable as a

lady could be, under the circumstances;
but, at the same time, wishing her and her
beautiful violet eyes at the Antipodes. A
vague doubt, most injurious to the lady,
did occur to him—it was a very odd thing
altogether, and particularly odd that she
should have slept so very soundly that all
the necessary noise of hoisting sails, and
all the bustle incident on a ship's departure
had not roused her.

"If Blanche hears of it, what in the
name of Heaven will she think? Well, if
ever a man was punished for a silly little
flirtation, I am that man."

He was not in the least disposed to run
off with any lady, but to be obliged to
have a lady run away with him was hard
indeed—and he felt himself much aggrieved. He conquered himself sufficiently
to behave with politeness to the fair Doña
Matilda, but not an iota more.

"I wonder," he thought, with an unflattering look of disgust, "whether the

lady has got some clean things in her pocket!"

If, in truth, a tender sentiment had anything to do with her adventure, it was most thoroughly ill-rewarded on Villeroy's part.

He gathered that she had friends at Lisbon, and thither he resolved to take her, and there to leave her, though most inconvenient to him, and causing a delay he would have grudged even for a pleasant purpose. Moreover, though of course respect sealed their lips, he could see that all the crew viewed the case as a romantic love affair. Provoking as it was, he could not assemble his men and make a public declaration—that so far from being desperately in love with Doña Matilda, he considered her being there a most intense bore.

Meanwhile the weather, though threatening and bad, did not as yet realize all the menace it had held out. It made poor

Doña Matilda very ill, and terrified her exceedingly, but it did not amount to serious danger. They made for Lisbon, and at last sighted the coast.

Villeroy had felt himself too much out of temper to talk in his usual good-natured, easy way to his Captain; but now Captain Warden himself came forward, and began a conversation with him.

"I suppose, Sir," he said, with a rather foolish smile, that Villeroy fancied it looked like an awkward attempt to banter, "you don't feel inclined for the lady to make the rest of the voyage with us?"

"Most decidedly not!" said Villeroy, looking as unamiable as it was in his power to look.

"Oh! you don't, Sir; you object to it?"

"Most decidedly," repeated Villeroy, bending his black brows into a frown.

"She is a nice lady too, and gives very little trouble; I'm sure, Sir, she speaks in the very pleasantest way of *you*, Mr. Ville-roy."

"I am much obliged to her," said Mr. Villeroy sarcastically.

There was a pause.

"I *had* thought, Sir," said Warden, "in Lisbon—a priest might easily be—it might be managed with very slight delay—the ceremony might take place."

"What ceremony?" asked Villeroy angrily.

"Well, Sir, of course, the marriage ceremony."

"Pshaw! are you mad?"

"The lady is beautiful, and has a fine fortune," said Warden, also a little hotly; "but of course it must be as you please."

"I should rather imagine so," said Villeroy, with a scornful laugh.

Captain Warden muttered some wrathful expression, and walked away in a rage.

Villeroy, angry as he was, could not help laughing.

" Rather good ; going off in a rage because I won't be married against my will !"

Captain Warden's anger never lasted;
and Villeroy, who had a sincere regard for
him, and did not wish to vex him, spoke
good-humouredly on some indifferent subject, and then said :

" Doña Matilda has friends, I believe,
at Lisbon ?"

" Yes, Sir," said Captain Warden, rather
stiffly, " very good friends—relations of
her late husband. It was only my idea—
knowing how busy evil tongues are, and
knowing how highly a lady values her good
name in the most trifling particular—that
the marriage might have taken place at
Lisbon as well as anywhere else, and thus
silence any ill-natured remarks."

Villeroy was greatly astonished at the
pertinacity of the man, and looked at his
flushed, displeased face in surprise, when
a new idea suddenly occurred to him.

" However, Sir," continued the honest

captain, " of course it must not be against your will. I came to you as a single man, and must return so, and go back to Lisbon to marry Matilda as fast as I can get there. You know that I, too, am a Roman Catholic, Sir."

Villeroy was struck dumb, utterly abashed at what he considered his own inconceivable stupidity and self-conceit.

" My dear Warden," he exclaimed, " pray forgive me. I must have been mad— dreaming. I congratulate you most sincerely ; of course, if you desire to marry the lady, I am most happy to accommodate you in every possible way."

" Surely, Sir, you never suspected me of any dishonourable thoughts !"

" Indeed, I know you too well. Pray think no more of it ; I was—really I don't know what I was."

Nor did Captain Warden care to find out. He was too happy to trouble himself with a single question, and Villeroy was almost as well pleased.

It was so fortunate a *dénouement*, that it obviated all difficulty, doubt, and suspicion; and he knew not how to be gallant enough to the fair Doña Matilda, or how to offer with sufficient cordiality all possible conveniences on board the *Ariel* for her voyage to England as Mrs. Warden.

Fearing lest it might be troublesome, Captain Warden made considerable scruples and ceremony as to accepting the offer to convey her home, but consented to do so with pleasure after a due and proper amount of pressing.

As to Doña Matilda, if she had ever entertained more ambitious prospects, the considerate kindness and warm-hearted politeness of Captain Warden during her involuntary cruise to Lisbon had entirely won her heart, and she bestowed it on him with her hand in all sincerity and affection.

One afternoon, a day or two after they

had left Lisbon, Doña Matilda, who did not like the boisterous weather that still followed them, was lying down in her cabin, as Villeroy and Captain Warden were conversing together on deck. The former was expressing the gratification he felt at Warden's prosperous marriage.

" You are a lucky fellow to get so pretty a wife, and so good a fortune, after all."

"Yes, Sir," said Captain Warden in slight embarrassment; " and something besides."

" What !" exclaimed Villeroy ; " you did not tell me what else."

" A baby, Sir—a little Portuguese baby. Don Antonio, Matilda's first husband, did not die childless ; not altogether, at least. The baby was born five months after he died, poor thing."

" Oh, indeed !" answered Villeroy. "When did you discover this addition to your family ?"

" Oh, the first day we were at Lisbon.

The first leisure hour we had, Matilda said she wanted me to go with her into the country. Of course I made no difficulty, so we got a sort of shandradan, and drove out among the vineyards till we came to a tidy stone cottage, where we got out, and Matilda ran in, and I after. There was a cradle standing on the stone floor, and by the side a decent, stout woman, and in it a baby. So Matilda pulled out the baby, and began kissing it. Then she said : ' This little darling is mine, and will be yours.' And she held it up to my lips."

" And what did you do ?" asked Villeroy.

" Why, Sir, I kissed it, and she standing by. It wasn't just what we should call in England a pretty baby. Its face was as yellow as a lemon, and not much bigger, and the biggest part of that were eyes— great black eyes. But that is a trifle, and I shall get used to it."

" And does she mean to leave the baby there ?" inquired Villeroy.

" Oh, by no means, Sir ; we shall go and
fetch it when the Summer comes on, and
the weather's more favourable. She
thought it too rough now. And she said
you mightn't like a baby on board—young
men not being always over-fond of babies ;
and indeed if she had not thought of that,
I should."

" Well, Captain Warden, to get a beautiful wife, and a fortune, and a ready-made
baby, you do come home a man of importance. I hope you'll like your Portuguese
baby."

" I'm sure I shall, Sir. I know with
dogs, I've always liked the ugliest best. I
dare say it will be something the same way
now. And you'll please, Sir, not to let out
to Doña Matilda that I didn't call it a
beauty ; for she says it's as lovely as an
angel, and the image of Don Antonio. It's
been out to nurse there for the benefit of
the country air, and she says that's what
makes it such a fine, beautiful baby. It's

near upon a year old, and it's all bound up
like a mummy, too. If she had not kissed
it first, it would have given me a bit of a
cold shudder to kiss the queer little thing.
But I daresay it will look more natural
when it's untied."

Villeroy laughed. He did feel very grate-
ful indeed to Doña Matilda for not bringing with her this additional passenger; to
come home laden with a lady and a baby
was something beyond his ambition.

CHAPTER VI.

THE clouds and storms that seemed to follow in the wake of the *Ariel* still continued to dog its path. The weather became more boisterous as they entered the Channel.

The morning broke dark and sullen; a cold white fog had to sustain a severe struggle with the sun that gleamed out at short intervals early in the day, but retired ere long behind a thick embankment of cloud and mist, while, as if in triumph, the winds roared and shrieked, and the waves leapt high against the sides of the vessel.

It was about noon, when the yacht,

under all the sail she could carry, was staggering along not far from the Isle of Wight, having left the Needles to leeward and astern. The weather had been getting more and more threatening since the morning, but in spite of the sensibly increasing gale the sail had been kept on, as Villeroy was determined if possible to reach Portsmouth, or at least Spithead, that night.

The little vessel was labouring heavily enough as it was, sometimes heeling over to an apparently dangerous degree, and occasionally plunging uneasily, as if determined to go through all the now heavy seas she met, instead of over them. Still all the gear held on promisingly, though the lee rigging appeared every time the craft felt the fresh force of the wind to bow before it, to hang loosely and in bights, until recovering herself, it tautened again with a jerk and snap that spoke well for its sea-worthiness.

The spray was continually dashing over in perfect showers of salt rain, forcing those on deck to seek such shelter as the low bulwarks afforded—a shelter, however that neither Villeroy, nor Captain Warden, nor the helmsman he was assisting could take advantage of.

It was plain enough, as they got along the coast, that should the wind not shift a point or two in their favour, with the heavy sea running, and every moment getting more and more angry, they could never hope to clear the St. Catherine's lighthouse point. They had got beyond Brooke by two o'clock, but they well knew that falling off the wind, as the yacht was doing every time a more than usually heavy sea struck her, their chance was getting less.

To make a tack to windward, and so get a better offing, was the only plan that suggested itself to the Captain's mind, as to wear the ship with the in-draught of the tide, especially with the well-known dangers of the Chale Bay undercurrent, would have been far too hazardous. Yet as it was, with the heavy canvas on her, not a rag of which he dared to take off, as it would have lessened the schooner's way and probably caused her to miss stays when he attempted to tack—she was working so heavily, and straining so much, that accidents to masts and spars, or leaks to the vessel could not but be looked for every moment.

In the meantime the sky had been getting more and more dark; the rain was now coming down with every fresh effort of the wind, which was blowing in alternate gusts and squalls, and mingling with the spray, which deluged the deck and blinded those on it. The horizon was invisible owing to the thick driving mist, which only cleared away now and then as the sudden blasts of wind drove it in sheets in the direction of the little craft,

and to leeward nothing was to be seen
but the great cliffs looming darkly and
frowningly out of the thick fog, bold and
terrible in their undefined forms, chilling
the hearts of those on board, who
knowing the fatal nature of the coast were
breathing prayers for the brave little
schooner's safety.

"She must go about now, Sir," said
Captain Warden to Villeroy, as they both
leaned their heads over the compass, watching by the card how much the ship's head
fell off at every heavy sea that struck her,
and still more at every plunge she gave
burying her handsome bows.

"Every moment we are getting more
and more in. And see, Sir!" he cried, as
the rain-mist cleared up for a moment,
"we have lost sight of St. Catharine's
Light, and we know—Heaven help us!—
that we cannot afford to lose a fathom of
ground in Chale Bay."

"I think," said Captain Warden, "from

the increasing strength of the squalls, that
we have got to the height of the gale."
And even as he spoke, one little blue patch
of sky appeared above, as if endorsing his
words. "And if the wind does but shift a
little, we can manage, I believe, but it will
be ticklish work. If," he resumed, after a
brief pause, "we *can* tack her, we might,
after getting her round, and gaining some
slight offing, get some of the canvas down;
but even should we fail, sea-room and no
spars is better than those ugly cliffs to leeward. Few men reach them alive in such
a sea as this."

"As you will," answered Villeroy; "but
it is a bitter disappointment not to get into
harbour to-night; and still more so if we
cannot get out of this danger. So close to
home, too! But we must do what we can.
Do you see any other sails about?"

"No, Sir," answered the helmsman, who
was peering to windward as well as the
drift would allow him. "But I thought I

saw something like a pilot-boat—a lugger, I think—on the weather-bow. They mostly cruise off here in dirty weather, to pick up homeward-bounders."

The Captain had gone forward to call all the men; not but that they were all on deck—the situation was by far too anxious a one to allow of their being below—but the operation of going about in so tautly rigged a vessel, and in such a sea, required precautions to which the good seaman was no stranger. He knew that by a few plain words of instruction to the men he could convey his meaning far better than by any hoarse words of command, which would have only mingled with the roar of the winds and waters, and most probably have been misunderstood.

In a few minutes all was ready—the Captain standing close to the helm, and Villeroy assisting the helmsman. The ship, by the direction of the Captain, was kept off a few points, to increase the way, and

so to assure her staying. Then at a glance
of the Captain's the helm was put down.
The moment was an anxious one, as the
ship's head had come slowly up to the
wind, dipping her sharp bows into the sea,
which seemed to send her back at every
plunge; the way that had been given her,
however, proved in her favour, and at last
she got head to wind. Had it been possible now to have taken in a reef, the crew
would have done so, before she filled on the
other tack, but she was far too short-
handed for that, and they reckoned to get
her under easier sail when she had fairly
breasted the offing.

"She is round now, thank Heaven!"
shouted the Captain to Villeroy. "Another
moment and the sails will fill. Mind your
helm, and don't let her run off too much!"
he cried, as the sails began to draw. "Here
comes—here comes something! Luff, Sir,
luff! Close to it, Sir. Hold on, men—
here it is!" shouted he, as a heavy squall

came down on them, making the very sea almost smooth before its advance.

Everyone caught something to hold on by, as the fierce wind reached the schooner. One cry burst from all lips as the blast struck the helpless vessel. There had been no time to shorten sail even before the squall. It takes her on the port side, just before the beam, the gallant little craft resists—she staggers over, rights again. Another reel over to leeward, a noise of flapping canvas, a shock like the report of a heavy cannon, a sudden sensation felt by all on board as if the deck were slipping from under their feet, and the squall is over.

The bright blue sky is again to be seen overhead, but the little yacht is on her beam ends.

As the squall struck her, the mainboom sheet had carried away bodily block-tackle and all, and jammed the boom against the lee main rigging, in itself enough to cap-

size a vessel; but in addition the fore-try-
sail sheet had also been carried away, and
then the two huge sails, far too large for so
small a craft, except in the true Mediterranean weather, leaning against the rigging
had forced her over; and there she lay
with almost half her deck buried in the
water, while at every move of the sea she
seemed to attempt to rise again; her lower
masts, indeed her only mast-heads (for the
little show poles she had at first in guise of
topmasts were carried away), rising a few
feet in the air, then drooping to the level
of the water again.

In one way, desperate as the situation
was, it was not hopeless; thanks to the
repeated cautions of the Captain, all had
managed to get hold of something to cling
by, so that no lives had been lost yet, still
their position was in the highest degree
dangerous. As if the wind, in its last efforts,
had mustered all its remaining force to des-
troy its little victim, and was now satisfied

with the mischief it had wrought, it began
to abate its strength—by no means an uncommon phenomenon of our south-easterly
gales at the back of the Isle of Wight. Yet
the sea was now again becoming heavier,
as if in rebellion to the superior force of
the wind, which had compelled it to appear
so calm while the squall lasted.

It chanced that Villeroy had managed to
secure himself to one of the boat's davits,
which afforded him a good support; and
when the first emotions of the shock were
over, his naturally cool head and presence
of mind in danger enabled him to
realize his position, and calculate the
means of escaping from it. But deep
beneath these feelings ran a strong
current of thought in a very different
direction—thoughts of Blanche—a wish
that for the last few days had been floating
in his mind, and that this last imminent
peril had brought more prominently into

view, and formed itself with greater firm-
ness and precision in his mind.

Captain Warden, always thinking of the
vessel under his charge before any more
private anxiety, had not given a thought
to his own personal danger. He knew that
their only chance was to get the vessel
righted, and there was but one way to do
that—and that was to cut away the masts.
Even then he knew she would be but a
helpless log on the water, but at that short
distance from land, he hoped it would not
be long ere assistance arrived. Still there
was the danger of getting swept into Chale
Bay by the undercurrent, and then what
chance of life was there among those dark
rocks and deep waters ?

His eyes, as they encountered those of
Villeroy, sufficiently showed his concern,
but in another moment the instinct, natural
to every thorough seaman that impels him
to work, to do something, returned to him,
and his glance brightened as he cast it

round the vessel's side, and noticed that not one of those who depended on his skill and courage for their lives were missing.

"Not one lost, thank God!" he cried. "Come, Sir, we shall do yet!"

Save the rising and falling on the waves the vessel was now tolerably steady, and thanks to the Captain's old man-of-war ideas—which, although they left him at full liberty to delight in the beauty and adornment of his little charge, yet always taught him to combine the useful with the ornamental—good stout riggers' axes had been fastened to the inside of the bulwarks.

With the aid of his loud clear voice, he managed to make his intentions known to the men, who one by one on conceiving his meaning, disengaged themselves from their holdings, and contrived to clamber on the exposed surface of the vessel's side —there was no getting to leeward to cut away the lee rigging, the water coming up almost to the combings of the hatchways;

but that could be done well enough if she
righted, and of the ship's doing so there
could be little doubt, as the principal cause
of her being held down in the water was
the great weight of her masts, and the
large sails caught against the lee rigging
being full of water.

The axes are soon reached; three men
for the foremast, three more for the main
—a few hard-cutting blows given together,
severing the rigging—a half roll to windward—a crash—then another—a hasty
clambering from the outside to the inside
of the bulwarks. She scuds to windward
once more—the masts are gone—the ship
upright—she is saved! One loud cheer of
victory, and the *Ariel* is upright, but unmanageable on the water !

In the face of matters as they were, there
was still considerable danger, and now that
the more immediate pressure on all their
feelings had passed, Villeroy taking the
risk into consideration determined to fulfil

the purpose that even amid the past turmoil had been working in his brain, and had now become a fixed determination. "At least," he thought, "if this is to be the end of it as far as I am concerned, Cecil and Blanche shall, if possible, be rescued from their unhappy position." The less probability there appeared of their ultimate safety, the greater became his anxiety on their account. In this hour of danger he thought more of her than of himself; he wondered at his own want of energy as he deemed it, in not having urged on her his love, his hopes, in words that could not have been withstood; how could such great love have been so weakly expressed? Had he spoken as he felt she might perhaps have now been his, and then had he died she would have been left at least above all worldly cares, rich and honoured.

Actuated by such thoughts as these, he took his opportunity to hurry down to his cabin, where amidst the wreck of furniture and broken glass he managed to find his desk, and quickly, but as clearly as he could, he wrote a short ducument, leaving by will to Blanche and Cecil his principal estate, Burton-Hassett, adding also a few lines to his mother; as he finished writing Captain Warden came out of the cabin beyond, he had run down for one moment to his wife.

"How is Doña Matilda?" asked Villeroy, kindly.

"She feels like dying," was the answer, "but she says she had rather be with me here than safe at Cadiz without me," and the bright eyes glistened.

"You will never forget this, Warden," said Villeroy, "I too have been thinking of my friends—will you put your signature to this?"

Warden did so without a comment, and one of the sailors who had come down to speak to Captain Warden, also added his.

Villeroy enclosed the papers in a bottle,

which he securely corked and sealed, having dropped in a few sovereigns for the finder of it, with directions where the packet was to be forwarded, and as he put it in the pocket of his pea-jacket, he experienced a strange sense of satisfaction and contentment. In that respect his mind was at ease. Blanche would receive a proof of his unutterable affection, and at the same time be rescued from a state of poverty she was neither born nor fitted to endure, rescued through his protecting care; and at this reflection his generous heart beat with the most utterly disinterested thankfulness that it was in his power so to demonstrate the love with which she had inspired him.

He then again hastened on deck, and glanced around. The clouds again seemed lowering, and he could discern through the haze low ridges of black rough rocks, while towards the shore, a vast sheet of snow-white foam seemed drawn to and fro by invisible hands.

Without farther delay he leaned forward and dropped the bottle over the vessel's side, praying that this silent messenger might yet speak his last words for him.

He had scarcely done so when salvation came; the very pilot boat they had seen before the squall struck the vessel, was observed standing towards them quickly, and ere long they were safely at anchor in Sandown Bay.

Contrary to their expectation the weather had cleared, and, a nice breeze from the westward having sprung up the pilot boat took them in tow, after rigging a jury-mast and setting a spare sail.

Villeroy landed in one of the fishermen's boats, and immediately proceeded to get a conveyance to Ryde, and from thence to Portsmouth, where he only remained long enough to give directions to Lloyd's people to send a tug to get his vessel round.

E 2

In London a letter was awaiting him from his mother, Lady Dornington, which compelled him, unwilling as he was, to join her at once at Hellingsley, before he was able to make inquiries, or take steps to seek out Blanche or Cecil; thus it was that he was still in ignorance of their present situation.

CHAPTER V.

MRS. BREWSTER, in one way or other, managed to pick up all the news of the neighbourhood, and had a great delight in imparting the information she obtained; therefore, whether she would or not, Blanche was made cognisant of most that was going on.

One day Mrs. Brewster had been giving her a description of the gay doings that were taking place at Squire Bingham's, an elderly, unmarried man of fortune; his relative, Lady Arrandale, and her two daughters, Lady Helen and Lady Georgina, were on a visit there, and Lady Georgina was a bride; not long since she had married a gentleman, who they said was about the richest in England, a Mr. Joking Martinez.

Blanche could not help giving a jump.

" Well, it do seem a queer name, Miss ; but so it is—leastways, so they call him, Mr. Joking Martinez."

Blanche then asked how long he had been married to Lady Georgina, and found that she must have given him her hand about a month after his breaking off the engagement with her; in fact, though she had not known it, he had been for some time balancing between herself and the connection with a title, before the misfortunes that had fallen on the Conways were known to him.

" And only think, Miss, what gay doings we are to have at the Abbey. A dinner-party to-day, and a hunt breakfast to-morrow ! why, poor Mrs. Arnicott is half out of her wits, she is not used to such bustling work."

" And are the bride and bridegroom to dine at the Abbey to-day?" inquired Blanche.

" Yes, ma'am, they are; and it's not to be later than six, 'cause my Lady Arrandale is a bit of an invalid."

" Is Lady Georgina pretty?" asked Blanche.

" Oh yes, ma'am! 'specially being my lady, and so rich! *rayther* dark or so; but some people like that—and very genteel—very genteel indeed—a little slight thing—what you call a nice, little brunette. I see her myself walking along the dirty roads, along with her sister, Lady Helen, with her dress looped up, and a pair of little boots about big enough for your kitten, Miss, and a round hat and feather. Lawk! why she looked just like any other nice little girl; you'd never have guessed she was married, and my lady—and rich enough to throw gold in the gutter!"

Blanche felt a great curiosity to see the bride of her former admirer, wondering whether she liked him, whether he made himself agreeable to her, and a hundred other things; all on a sudden she determined to have a look at her. At a certain part of the road they had to pass, a path crossed it with a high stile, behind which Blanche could stand without the least risk of being noticed.

She came to the stile only a minute before the carriage came dashing along at a good pace, followed by a second; for Lady Arrandale seemed to prefer the company of her favourite lady's-maid to that of her son-in-law, and chose to drive in the latter conveyance.

It was but a moment, still Blanche saw all distinctly—Mr. Joachim Martinez and his bride in the front seat, and Lady Helen with her back to the horses.

Mr. Martinez and Lady Georgina were looking out at the opposite windows, fortunately Lady Georgina was on the side where Blanche stood. She saw clouds of lace and showers of diamonds, and a pretty little brunette face in the midst, very much like the little brunette face opposite of Lady Helen.

" I wonder," thought Blanche, "whether Lady Helen sits there to have more room for the sweeping skirts, looped up with bouquets of snowdrops and crocus, or whether Mr. Joachim Martinez prefers to have the best seat himself. How very absurd! I ought to have been sitting there on those blue satin cushions, but I don't know that I had not rather be as I am ; she is just what Mrs. Brewster says— a nice little thing. I hope she won't be unhappy !"

With these thoughts, and a mixture of odd sensations she hardly understood, she returned to the Lodge.

" I hope Cecil will not see him," she said to herself. " Not likely," she added, for it seemed that they had been at Mr. Bingham's some little time, and meant to leave that part of the country soon after the hunt-breakfast, which was to take place at Holland Abbey the following day.

CHAPTER VI.

O N Wednesday, at ten o'clock, the handsome banqueting-hall at Holland
Abbey was rapidly beginning to fill; men
chiefly in hunting costumes; ladies, dark,
fair and brown, in velvets, satins, moirés
antiques of every hue and every shade, sat
down to a brilliant repast. The tables, in
the shape of a T, were loaded with all that
can be thought of or imagined at such col-
lations, glittering with silver, glass, china,
and gold; the dishes interspersed with
tall épergnes, statuettes, gold and silver
cups, confectionery temples, and pyra-
mids of hot-house flowers.

Everyone was smiling, talking, or eat-

ing; yet if we could put on a pair of
moral spectacles, we should see that all
was not, alas! so happy below the surface.

Mrs. Talbot wondered why Lord William
took Mrs. Effingham out before her, "and
quite in a marked way too — almost a
pointed slight." She did not perceive that
Mrs. Effingham was a pleasant, good-
natured woman, and she the reverse. Miss
Harriet Slingsby thought, "How very tire-
some; there is George Henley, who was
so civil and attentive to me at the ball,
sitting next that Miss Clifford, who has
nothing in the whole world except a complexion and a pair of eyes. What was the
use of teazing mamma into taking me, when
she said it was too many to bring five, even
to a hunt-breakfast? I had much better
have stayed at home!"

Then there was the widowed Lady Hillham, who had spent a quarter of a year's
pension on Anna Maria's beautiful silk and
her velvet cloak; and after all, her bonnet

was unbecoming, she had a red nose, "and on the whole," said wretched Lady Hillham to herself, "I never saw her look so plain."

And there is a doting mother looking at her pretty Carry, and in spite of all she sees around her, the image of another idolized one, who only two short years before drooped and faded away in consumption, appears before her; and by an unhappy twist of the imagination, which occurs at such times as these, she views again the fragile form propped up by pillows, and hears the laboured breathing; and as she gazes at her last living darling, she thinks there is a shade too much of flush on the cheek, or a tint too pale, and she begins to think the afternoon will turn chilly and she had better not have come.

Those ancient Egyptians who found it necessary to place a skeleton at their feasts must have been jovial fellows to require it; we take care to bring our skeletons with us; yet Heaven forbid but that some on whom the hand of care did not press too heavily, and who were blessed with cheerful tempers, were happy and entered into the gaiety of the moment—some whose spirits were light, who became animated with the pleasant excitement, and were pleased to see old friends and new acquaintances. At all events everyone appeared pleased, veiling their private vexations; and such reticence is not hypocrisy—it is a necessary discretion—or our social meetings would be even more dull and cold than they generally are.

As the hour advanced, some of the more eager sportsmen began to look privately at their watches; some loiterers came in late, and others, without sitting down at all, took a hurried sandwich or glass of liqueur at the sideboard. Then there was a general move, the large body gradually poured forth and left the noble hall, the still loaded tables, and the rows of chairs all empty.

The morning was exactly what it ought to be for a hunt-breakfast, "a southerly wind," though not a cloudy sky; white clouds were sailing gaily across the azure, and bursts of sunshine and light shadows passed alternately over the landscape. The wide stone terrace in front of Holland Abbey looked from a little distance like a bed of variegated tulips, for the ladies stood there in their gay costumes to have a view of the field, while the court-yard and wide entrance-drive were lined with carriages of every description, landaus, dog-carts, broughams, saddle-horses, grooms, and small boys in livery, all in high spirits and good humour.

On the broad green slope opposite, a cluster of men in scarlet had already collected around the huntsman and the hounds, while bright red spots, where the sun shone on them, showed other hunting men joining the group from different directions.

The magnates of the hunt now came dropping in leisurely, their careless, easy demeanour in the midst of the bustle bespeaking them veterans in the field. Sir Phillip Holland, though he did not mean to hunt, also rode down on a splendid, large bay, high-spirited, but as tractable as a lamb, his master looking a very handsome and dignified man, very different from the rough character he often chose to appear. On these occasions he was courteous to all, though he still maintained a slight tone of superiority.

Near him rode two pretty young girls, Lady Helen Arrandale and the bride, Lady Georgina Martinez, on whose other side was Mr. Joachim Martinez, conspicuous on a tall, magnificent grey, which happened to be on that day the only grey horse out. His spick and span new scarlet, dazzlingly white cords, and perfect get-up, with his black whiskers and well-cut aquiline nose, gave him a very imposing appearance, which circumstance he was well aware of. He frequently turned those sharp, black eyes of his on his pretty bride; for, truth to tell though he might not be fond of her, he was undeniably jealous. It was disagreeable to him if a good-looking man paid her the attentions due to a young and charming bride. Some of the ladies thought him handsome—the men could not endure him.

As so much delay had been already occasioned by the breakfast, Sir Philip thought it but right when they did once emerge from the house, that the patience of the sportsmen who had not had the *entrée* should be no farther tested; so they trotted off at once to a wood about a mile and a half distant, which to Mr. Martinez's infinite delight, who was no great rider, was drawn blank. Not so, however, a beautiful covert on the sunny slope of a hill, about two miles further on, for no sooner had the hounds dashed in than challenge after challenge was heard, till the whole pack opened in full chorus, and a fine sleek fox, who had evidently been living on rather more intimate terms with the numerous rabbits in the vicinity than they perhaps fully approved of, was only too thankful to break away, as it was getting all too hot to hold him. Then burst forth the cheering view holloa—the horn of the huntsman—the " gone away " of the whips, addressed in reproof to the lagging hounds, and all the glorious excitement of a splendid find.

Over the hills, down the slopes, along the valleys, away they go. But now the fox makes for the open moor-land and all are on his track, the scent is warm and only a few stragglers remain behind.

There was one spectator who was not only interested, but highly excited by this lively scene. Cecil had been looking on, and now forgetting all his duties, quite carried away by the love of the sport which is inherent in all young Englishmen who are not reading men, off he ran at full speed to keep sight of them, while all his frame quivered with the eager longing he felt to be among them. His great passion, perhaps his foible, was the love of horses, and a hunting-field was to him something very like Elysium.

It was not possible to keep long in view the whole field, and soon all seemed to have melted away, when his attention was arrested by the appearance of a small group, who evidently not knowing the country, were taking a very wrong direction towards some high broken downs, most dangerous for horses, not only because they were full of grips and mounds, but because they were broken by a ragged, winding ravine; and in many places, especially where these riders seemed to

be going, the loose ground and turf over-
hung the sides in such a manner that it
was not observable till you were close
upon it, and if the horses were galloping,
would probably not be noticed in time to
check them.

Though little disposed to address any
of the party, he felt compelled to hasten
forward and give the requisite warning,
especially as two of the three were ladies,
evidently under the care of the very dandy
man on a fine grey horse, whom Cecil had
before remarked as being a bad rider;
indeed Joachim Martinez, for it was he,
was glad of the excuse of lingering near
his young wife, rather than following the
break-neck course which the others were
taking.

Before Cecil reached them he recognized
Martinez, the man of all others he most
disliked. At that very moment Lady
Georgina's mare, much too spirited an
animal for a slight young girl to manage,

took fright at some birds, or something in the furze bushes, and set off at a furious gallop, totally uncontrolled and unmanageable.

Joachim Martinez did the very worst thing possible, by setting off in pursuit of her; the loud, heavy tramp of his horse's feet on the elastic turf, adding to the excitement of the frightened animal— not for long, however, for his grey stumbling from catching his hoof in a rift, threw him headlong, though he still grasped the bridle that he had been clutching with all his power. In a moment Cecil was by his side, releasing him from the bridle; he saw at a glance that Martinez was not seriously hurt, though scared and bewildered.

"The brute!" exclaimed Martinez, "my shoulder's out, I'll be sworn it is," rising and looking round, "I can't mount the brute again."

"Then let me," said Cecil, a little roughly.

"Where can I go? Where am I to get help?"

Cecil threw his arm contemptuously in the direction he had come from, where Martinez remembered that they had passed shortly before a small, lonely farm-house in a little gully, and thither he bent his steps, while Cecil in one moment was in the saddle, and the next urging the grey to his full speed, leaping over furze bushes, skirting round the high heaps of stones, avoiding impracticable spots and lifting him over difficult ones, as only a good rider can; but not, like Martinez, straight behind the heels of the terrified mare, though he constantly kept her in sight as she went winding in and out, up and down, and the blood rushed to his heart as he saw her making straight for the edge of the ravine.

He guided his brave horse to its very

rim, still galloping along its verge so as to intercept the mare at an angle more or less obtuse whenever the last critical moment should arrive, as it were warding her off the fatal precipice. One false step of the good grey, one sudden swerve, one shy at any startling object would have sent him and his rider down the rough sides of the chasm. Cecil saw the danger, but felt not the slightest fear of the risk. He believed himself to be thoroughly master of his horse; he had that power, half the result of skill and practice, half of instinct, that enables Blondin to walk fearlessly on the tightened rope. All his thoughts were how best to arrest the flight of the animal whose devious course showed signs of failing strength; he admired too the courage of the girl who still retained her seat. At last the moment came, and holding in his horse to a moderate degree, he confronted the mare not a dozen yards from the overhanging edge of the cliff, and seizing her by the bridle, turned her head in the opposite direction.

Lady Georgina had indeed found it difficult to support herself against her own fears, as well as from the effect of the violent exertion of such a race over such ground. Her strength was just failing her, her breath came short, her hand trembled, when on a sudden she beheld what was likely to be the fearful termination of her course; she perceived before her, almost below her, the ravine, and almost at the same instant, she saw dimly and with failing eyes—but the image was ineffaceably impressed on her imagination—the tall grey with his long strides, and the rider, who she never once doubted was her husband; she saw his imminent peril as well as her own, for at moments of extreme danger the perceptions seem quickened— she saw all, but as in a thick mist, and then all was dark before her eyes.

Happily the mare, almost exhausted as

she was, submitted herself quietly to the
hold of Cecil; had it been otherwise the
success of his act might have been doubtful,
but she passively suffered herself to be
managed by him as he would, and stood
with panting sides, quivering ears and
snorting nostril, but motionless. He was
certain from her wild, rolling eye and
entire appearance, that she was not a fit
animal for a delicate young girl to ride,
and probably was only half broken in.

He also perceived that Lady Georgina
was sinking in a fainting fit from her saddle,
and springing off the grey, throwing his
bridle over his arm, was but just in time
to save her from falling, by receiving her
in his arms. As he stood in some perplexity
how to contrive to take care of two horses
and an insensible girl, he mentioned the
name of Mr. Joachim Martinez in no flattering terms—fool and brute being perhaps
the least objectionable.

As he looked round he saw that the

mists were gathering, and it had turned cold and raw ; the farm-house whither Mr. Martinez had repaired was now at least two miles distant, and he doubted whether he should be able to carry the young lady so far over the difficult ground, to say nothing of the care of his two horses.

He all at once remembered a forlorn and not very reputable public-house somewhere near, and looking anxiously about, caught sight of it, at a very short distance from where he stood.

He perceived that his only course was to release the filly, leaving her to her own devices, and leading the grey behind him to carry Lady Georgina to the small inn. The good creature followed him as gently as a dog; so he proceeded with his burden as fast as he could, being very desirous to place her where necessary warmth and restoratives could be administered.

CHAPTER VII.

HAVING described the situation of all except Lady Helen, it ought to be mentioned that she, struck dumb with alarm at the danger of her sister, had sat immoveable until she saw Martinez thrown. Not very fond of her new brother-in-law, she beheld him with unfeigned scorn and indignation, selfishly forgetting all but himself, betake himself to his homeward path, deserting her sister and leaving her to the mercy of a stranger; then she advanced though at a cautious pace, well knowing that she could render no assistance, until she, too, suddenly beheld the dangerous ravine winding here and there opposite her. Paralysed with horror she checked her horse, and remained long enough to see Cecil's well-managed rescue; when she trotted at a brisk pace towards the public-house, which she also had caught sight of, to procure assistance.

She rode quickly up to the high narrow door, and knocked loudly with her riding whip; it seemed very long before she could bring anyone, but at last a shaggy, dirty, down-looking man partly opened the door and stared at her.

"Let me in," she said, "send some one —quick—"

The man looked back within the house, then the door opened and a hard-featured woman came forward.

"What do you want?" was the uncivil welcome.

"Is not this an inn? I want to come in, I want help—here—make haste some one, I've plenty of money."

An eager, unpleasant look crossed the woman's face.

" Oh ! come in—do, Miss," and with un-expected rapidity she was ushered into a close, wretched little parlour where it was nearly dark.

" Make a fire please, as soon as possible."

" Oh, yes, we'll make a fire."

And the woman went out, but did not soon return; Lady Helen ran impatiently to the door, tried to open it and found it locked.

A cold panic came over her, and a thought of terror for the first time crossed her mind. " They are going to rob, perhaps to murder me." She recalled the extreme loneliness of the place, the approaching darkness, the ravine. " How easily they could take me and throw me down that ravine—even if the man does come here with Georgina, he may come too late."

She flew to the window, but it was very hard to open. It was so long since it had been moved, that the little clumsy sash seemed stuck fast to the frame-work; but using her whole strength she succeeded at last, and called as loudly as she possibly could. In a minute or two the door opened, and the woman came in with kindling, as she called it, to light the fire. Whether they had any evil intentions it was not easy to say, but one of her sons, an unkempt lad of eighteen, had just run in and told her that people were coming across the downs to their cottage.

"What did you make a noise for?" asked the woman in a surly tone.

"Why," said Lady Helen angrily, "you had locked me in."

"Well, what o' that? My Becky is silly-like, a poor, daft thing, she might ha' come in and frightened you, she's mighty curious and prying about strangers."

"Well, don't do so again," said Lady Helen, "I've friends coming here—I expect them here every minute, they will be frozen in this cold place."

And she ran and knelt on the hearth, blowing as hard as she could with her pretty lips to make the fire blaze.

"And have you got some hot water, and something hot—like brandy, or some of those things? do run about a little, and get what we want."

"You're a pretty, confident little Miss," muttered the woman, rising however to do as she was desired.

Lady Helen went to the window, and saw Cecil approaching the door-way carrying her sister in his arms. Helen ran out to meet and usher them in; as they passed into the little room, Lady Georgina, who had somewhat revived, much to the surprise of Cecil, gently slipped her arm round his neck.

"Dear Joachim, I did not know you were so brave, forgive me, dearest," and before he or Lady Helen was able to interpose a word, she embraced him.

Lady Helen made him a rapid sign to be silent, placing her finger on her lips, and together they laid Lady Georgina on the narrow, hard, horse-hair sofa, when she again relapsed into a fainting state.

"Hush!" whispered Lady Helen. "She thinks it is her husband. Pray—pray do not undeceive her!"

"No, of course not," he answered.

"Tell them to bring some hot something and water," she said, hurriedly; and kneeling down, she pulled off her sister's boots, and began to rub her feet, for she was as cold as an icicle.

Finding the people of the house most disobliging and unwilling to assist, Cecil came in with the hot brandy and water; and with a tea-spoon Lady Helen gave it to her sister, who swallowed it with closed eyes. Just then the rumble of some conveyance was heard. Cecil looked out of the small square-paned window, and through

the darkening air saw a farmer's gig, driven
by a stupid, open-mouthed boy, and Mr.
Joachim Martinez descending from it.

On reaching the farmhouse he had found
himself so much less hurt than he supposed
that he bethought him of his little wife, and
after some slight delay procured the farmer's
gig, and the particularly stupid boy who
drove it. From this intelligent youth, who,
it appeared, had seen the whole adventure,
he understood that the " gentleman as
rode the grey 'oss had carried the gal "—
as he unpolitely named her—" to Sam
Hearney's public."

" Carried her—how ?"

" With his two arms," said the boy, with
a hazy wonder how else he should have
carried her.

Fretful and fuming, Mr. Martinez entered
hastily the mean little passage of the public-
house, and was encountered at the door by
Cecil coming out. Of course Mr. Joachim

Martinez would not yield the *pas,* and Cecil being less disposed to do so, a severe shock was the result as they jostled roughly against each other.

Martinez, who was the least prepared for so unceremonious a meeting, came spinning into the room, almost losing his balance.

" —— the fellow !" he cried, turning round in a rage ; but Lady Helen flew forward and arrested him.

" He has just saved Georgina's life, at great risk to himself ; and listen," she said, in a lower voice. " She thinks it was you. I advise you to allow her still to believe so."

" Pshaw—pooh !" began Mr. Martinez.

" You had better—most innocently she showed that she so believed it."

" What do you mean ?" he asked, fiercely.

" Oh, never mind, but she did. You may as well have the credit of a gallant act, and not distress Georgina by disclosing her mistake."

Martinez came moodily to the sofa and looked at her.

" By Jove ! she looks very ill. By Jove ! she's dying !"

" Don't frighten her—she may hear you. She is only faint; she will be better soon. But surely you intend to reward the brave man who saved her. It would be an eternal disgrace if you did not."

" Well," said Martinez, pulling out his purse, " take what you think proper, and give it him from me."

Lady Helen seized it, and ran after Cecil, with rather a merry smile on her lips.

" I will give him the purse just as it is. Mean as he is, he will not dare find fault. How enraged he will be—a stingy fellow !"

Much tickled and delighted with her intended trick on her niggardly brother-in-law, she came up to Cecil, who was striding away in no very good humour,

" Oh ! stop," she said, " stop a minute !"

Cecil immediately did so, with the polite,
indescribable look and manner of a perfectly well-bred man, and Lady Helen felt
a momentary embarrassment and doubt.

" Pray, pray do not suppose I can fancy
that such courage and generosity as you
have shown can be rewarded, but my
brother-in-law desired me to beg you to
accept this ;" and she held out the purse.

" Thank you," he answered in his natural,
gentlemanly voice, " but I cannot; it is
quite impossible—quite."

" Oh ! I am so sorry ; but you are not
offended ?"

" No, indeed ; the last thing I could be.
I thank you much for your kind intention."

" You understand," said Lady Helen,
" that my sister mistook you for her husband, who had been just before mounted
on that grey horse ?"

" Perfectly," said Cecil, " and I trust
you will not feel the slightest uneasiness ;

I assure you, upon my honour, that no word will ever pass my lips relating to what has passed in any way whatever. I hope she will continue to suppose it was her husband, and never be undeceived."

Helen felt touched by conduct so thoroughly generous and gentlemanly; she would have been more so if she had known that Cecil really disliked the man in question more than any other in the world— far more than Stephen Granville—even more than Orlando Henshawe, because there his dislike was greatly diluted by a feeling of the man's insignificance.

Lady Helen stood hesitating a minute, pulling to and fro a costly diamond ring she wore, the gift of her sister, and the only valuable ornament she possessed. She was just as liberal as Martinez was the reverse; she could not bear him to go without a mark of their gratitude. At last she said:

"You cannot refuse a lady's gift and

disappoint me; pray accept this from Lady Helen Arrandale."

What could he do but bow low and receive it?

" Is there anything I can do?" he asked.

" Nothing more," she replied, " but allow me to offer once again ten thousand thanks;" and Cecil resumed his way towards the lodge, while Helen returned to the public-house.

" Well," said Martinez, meeting her at the door, " what did you give him?"

" Of course your purse was what I offered; I could not think of offering less."

" My purse! my whole purse! why, you must be mad! My whole purse to a wandering vagabond because he had a lucky ride! You are strangely ignorant of the value of money; you take a little too much upon yourself."

" What do you mean, I should like to know?" exclaimed Lady Helen in a towering passion; "there's your paltry purse! *he* was a gentleman and did not care for it!" and she threw it down for him to pick up.

He knew it would not do to quarrel with Lady Helen, who was, he considered, a little spitfire.

"Well, Helen, I beg your pardon, but really your jokes are carried sometimes a little too far. I suppose the gentleman intends to blazon his heroic deed all over the country."

"No," said Lady Helen, "he gave his honour not to say a single word, and I know he will not."

Martinez went out into the yard, and addressed the stupid boy, who would, undoubtedly, have sat ruminating in his gig all night otherwise.

"Here, boy! go to the nearest place and send a close carriage here for me—to Sir Philip Holland's; or, if there is a nearer place, go there; but mind I must have a close carriage—do you understand, stupid?"

"Iss; you wants a close carriage," said the boy.

"Yes, and here's a half-crown, and if you're quick about it you shall have another half-crown—if you can get it," he added, muttering.

Gold will brighten the dullest intellect, and silver too; so the boy started off at a pace that put the respectable old horse he drove quite out of all his reckonings; and Mr. Martinez returned to the parlour, where, by this time, a good fire was blazing, and Lady Georgina was sitting upon the sofa.

"Oh, Joachim! I never, never shall forget what you did to-day—so brave, so heroic!"

Martinez winced; the very word he had himself applied ironically.

"Never mind, dear Georgina, think of something else—it agitates you."

" No, but I can't! oh! when I saw you galloping along there through the mist, almost like a phantom rider—in such danger—so brave—so courageous! you looked quite a hero! I never saw you look so noble before, and so beautifully done—though I was half gone, I saw it all. Oh! I would not have missed seeing you then for all the world! you dear Joachim! I am so sorry I have been cross sometimes!" and she drew him down to her on the sofa, petting him.

He felt a little discomfort at receiving these undeserved praises and ill-earned caresses, while Helen could scarcely help laughing.

" But what a mercy it is as it is," said Helen to herself; " if he had not been so thoroughly gentlemanly, and had gone and spread about the story. Good gracious! it would have been all over London, and we should not dare to show our faces. Such a history as they would have made of it!

nobody would have believed it was the harmless thing it was—the truth would have been nothing; but with all the additions and inventions, what would have been the end of it? If old Mrs. Hammerton or Lady Martindale had got hold of it! she is always calling us flirts, and fast, and all sorts of wicked things!"

CHAPTER VIII.

IN due time Martinez and Lady Georgina,
with Lady Helen, were installed in one
of the Holland Abbey carriages, and con-
veyed thither in safety.

They dined later than usual that evening, and Lady Georgina was so entirely
recovered that, against the wish of Joachim
Martinez, who tried to persuade her to
dine upstairs, she would come down.

"My dear, sweet Georgina," he urged,
"you don't know how pale you look, you
will really be ill, do stay up in your dress-
ing-room. If you are dull I will stay
with you."

"How very kind you are, dear Joachim!

but I would not—no, not for the world.
Mamma says they are all ringing your
praises, I would not miss it for anything.
I will go down to dinner, so that's
decided."

Accordingly down she came, in a bright
pink silk, with opals and diamonds, just
like a rose all over dew-drops, and every
one crowded round to congratulate her on
her escape.

"Oh! if it had not been for Joachim,"
she said, "I should never have heard these
kind words! no one can imagine how
dreadful and brave it was of him!"

For once in his life Joachim Martinez
was popular; he received all compliments
with a rather moody air. Some said,

"Really, after all I suppose Joachim
Martinez is modest!"

Others said:

"Well, if he rode as she describes, it
must have been a honeymoon inspiration!

for at other times he sits like a dragoon recruit."

" Miraculous power of love ! by George ! Lady Georgina is pretty enough to inspire a tailor."

Sir Philip Holland himself provoked Martinez most intensely by his overdone and slightly satirical praises.

All dinner time Lady Georgina's eyes beamed on him kindly, while Lady Helen sedulously averted hers.

" I give you my word, Lady Helen," said young Melford, a capital rider, and great sportsman, " I should have thought the whole thing a dream, a beatific vision of Lady Georgina's in some hour of transport, but that you too saw it all, did you not ?"

" Yes," answered Lady Helen.

" And it was all as it is described ?"

" Exactly," she asserted.

" A really plucky thing."

" Most undoubtedly."

"Well then," said Melford, "I'm sure I beg Martinez's pardon, for I could scarcely have believed it of him."

"Why not?" inquired Lady Helen.

"Oh! because—because he seems more of a lady's man."

"No, thank you," interrupted Lady Helen, "not that."

Melford looked at her, and they both laughed.

"There's something pulling the strings behind the scenes," said Melford.

"Mr. Melford, I am surprised at you!" said Lady Helen, in affected anger.

"Well, for a man who has just done that sort of thing, he is less self-satisfied than anyone I ever knew. I suspect it was you who rode the grey horse, Lady Helen."

"Why not say the grey mare at once?" interposed old Lord Burney, who was a privileged person at whom no one took offence. Lady Helen attacked him gaily in return, not sorry to turn the conversation.

The half-hour before the men went into the drawing-room was even more disagreeable to Martinez than the dinner. That short space of time was long enough for him to conceive a violent dislike to young Melford, who took pleasure in asking him what he considered impertinent questions; more especially as Melford was only heir to two thousand a year, and he was to be a millionaire.

"I say, Martinez," he inquired, "how did you feel when you were riding along the edge of that rough-looking grip—eh?"

"I felt as if I was on horseback," answered Martinez, curtly, and bit his lips.

He was now committed. It was the first direct admission he had made that he had done what was ascribed to him. Now, whether he would or not, he was bound to adhere to it.

A thousand questions perplexed and

worried him, as he sat in the drawing-room in an easy chair in the back-ground, affecting to look over a pamphlet. Suppose the real man were to come forward, and claim the acknowledgment of the act? Well, he must buy him off; for he had unlimited reliance on the power of money. No one had seen him at the farm-house, fortunately, except the stupid boy. The master was out, and he had declined going into the house. " And if that oaf were to say I drove in his gig, what then? It would only be a question of time. I might have gone there after taking Georgina to the public-house. I saw no one at the inn. No; it was most improbable it should ever come to light. After all, it was entirely Helen's doing."

Thus it was that Mr. Martinez became a hero. Blanche—who a few months ago, had she been near, would have been the belle and queen of the party at Holland Abbey—was hid in a little cottage beneath the shadow of the big house; and Cecil, who had risked his life, got a diamond ring that a chivalrous sentiment on his part prevented him from making any use of.

CHAPTER IX.

THOUGH Martinez now felt safe, and became reconciled to his new character, he was not over-delighted when he found that Lady Georgina had accepted Sir Philip Holland's invitation to finish her week at the Abbey; a most unusual act of grace on Sir Philip's part.

"I should soon get tired of them," he said to himself, "but for a few days I like it —they are two bright little goldfinches, and it's pleasant to have them twittering and chirping at my windows."

To complete Sir Philip's satisfaction, Martinez, who complained of his shoulder, declined hunting, and spent the greater part of his day at Mr. Bingham's, from a motive that would scarcely have influenced any man in his position except himself.

He was very desirous that he should leave something to Lady Georgina; it would have been but a grain of sand to him, yet he was as eager for it as if he were a poor man, " and," he said to himself, " why shouldn't he? people like to leave money to rich men, and hate to leave it to those who want it There is a powerful magnet in gold; gold attracts gold—and if I've married a girl with scarcely a sixpence, he ought to make it up to me."

Therefore he went to old Mr. Bingham's, praised his farming, stumped about his turnip-fields in varnished boots, asked his opinion and consulted him on subjects that he understood much better himself—in short if he had been a poor man, he might be said to toady the unsuspicious, hearty, old country gentleman.

Cecil returned towards the Lodge with a curious contrariety of feelings. He had experienced an all but irresistible desire as he jostled against Martinez, to turn back, whirl him by the arm out of the room, and do—he hardly knew what—but certainly nothing that would have been agreeable to Joachim Martinez; but with the ladies there it was impossible; moreover, as he reflected, it would have been the last thing he desired to make himself known to that gentleman.

Then those two pretty girls! the one he had carried in his arms—he did not allow his thoughts to wander beyond; and the other, who had so gracefully given him her ring.

But in a few minutes his fancy reverted to a different ride he had once had with Rosamond. He smiled as he thought of her alarms, he recollected her leaning so confidingly on him, and above all the engaging look she gave as she patted

Zuleika, begging her pardon in a way to fascinate man and horse.

So it happened that on re-entering the Lodge, he almost forgot the diamond ring in his waistcoat pocket.

Blanche ran out to meet him.

"Why, Cecil! I thought you were never coming! Have you got the key of the caddy? I am sure you have. I can't find it anywhere."

"This is the fifth time you have accused me of stealing the key of the caddy, Blanche; what a mercy it would be if the caddy had no key."

"That only shows your ignorance, Cecil; how could I be a housekeeper without keys, I should like to know?"

"Or without losing them?" suggested Cecil.

"You are an impertinent boy," laughed Blanche, diving her fingers into his waistcoat pocket before he knew what she was doing; "you young sinner! you have got it," she exclaimed, pulling out his diamond ring. " Why, Cecil, I never saw this pretty ring before !"

" No," said Cecil ; " well, I dare say I have rings, and studs, too, that you have not seen. I found a set of turquoise studs in a waistcoat pocket the other day, perhaps they'll do for you ;" and he went towards the door to fetch them, anxious to avoid further questioning.

" Oh ! stop a minute ; but this is a lady's ring ; how did you get it ? is it a *gage d'amour ?*"

" No, certainly not," Cecil answered.

" Then a *gage d'amitié ?* Come, tell me your secrets. Where did you get it ? was it in London ?"

" No," he answered.

" Then in Paris ? Oh ! do tell me ; why not ?"

" It is not fair to tell everything," he said ; " only I give you my honour it has nothing to do with love."

" How odd !" said Blanche ; " do I know the lady ?"

" If it were a lady—no, you do not."

" Well," said Blanche, " you're a shabby fellow not to tell me ; and to punish you, I will wear the ring."

" I would give it you with pleasure, but . . . ."

" Oh ! I shan't keep it ; you shall have it back ; but see, it just fits me !" and she held out her pretty white hand, laughing.

Cecil did not like to say much about it, for it was embarrassing to him, but he certainly did wish Blanche would not wear the ring.

" And your tea-caddy ?" he asked.

" Oh dear ! I don't know ; the key must be somewhere."

" I suppose so," said Cecil ; and as he spoke, Sally entered with the tray, and the tea made.

" Where was the key ?" asked Blanche.

" With your gloves, ma'am, on the bed."

Of course, as things generally do go wrong, it happened that Cecil and Blanche took a walk together the next afternoon in the wide alley that Blanche was very fond of; and so it was that Lady Georgina and Lady Helen took a quiet stroll together, after their four o'clock cup of tea, before they dressed for dinner, and entered a narrow riding that led into the very alley where Cecil and Blanche were lingering.

Blanche had taken her gloves off, and put them into her pocket, perhaps to tease Cecil by the sight of the mysterious ring that she still wore, and Cecil felt really a little annoyed that she would not give it up to him, and also in considerable dread lest by any chance it should be seen; yet he hardly liked to insist, for he found it difficult to parry Blanche's questions.

"I wish, Blanche, you would be a good girl and give me my ring; I have put the turquoise studs on your dressing-table."

" What, to buy me off! no, not yet—not till you tell me something about it."

" Don't think me cross, Blanche, but it really annoys me."

" Oh, if you're serious—there then."

And she held it out to him.

As ill-fortune would have it, Lady Georgina and Lady Helen at that juncture turned out of their little path into the riding where Blanche and Cecil stood, unseen by them.

Lady Georgina had in the morning asked Helen what she had done with her ring; and receiving no satisfactory answer, concluded that she had lost it and was ashamed to own it. But now she caught the sparkle of the diamond, as Blanche offered it to her brother, and feeling certain it was the missing ring—remembering also that they had several times walked in the alley before them, she had not a doubt that the two persons she now saw had found it and picked it up.

"Oh, Helen!" she exclaimed, "I am sure that is your ring. The man seems to be a gamekeeper."

And before Helen knew what to say, she came up to Cecil and Blanche and asked in her naturally polite manner if they had happened to pick up a diamond ring.

"Pray excuse me if I am mistaken, but I thought I saw you pick it up."

Cecil coloured deeply, at a loss what to say; but Lady Helen would not allow him for a moment to feel in a dilemma.

"No," she interposed; "I gave it to him. Pray forgive my rudeness, but I do not know your name?" she said, in an inquiring tone.

"You gave it him, and do not even know his name!" exclaimed Lady Georgina, in unbounded amazement.

"The name we are known by here is Crawford," said Blanche, calmly, for she was always equal to the occasion. "Our reason for concealing our own is a perfectly harmless one, I assure you; but we are very anxious that our secret should be preserved."

"It is safe with us," exclaimed Helen, "you may trust us both; and I am too deeply indebted to Mr. Crawford not to be anxious in every possible way to act in the manner he desires. But," she added, looking at Blanche, "I am certain that you are a lady, and——"

She glanced at Cecil.

"My brother," put in Blanche.

"And your brother a gentleman," continued Lady Helen, with a rapid glance from one to the other. "I mean by birth as well as in every other respect."

"But," exclaimed Lady Georgina, in the greatest amazement, "we are almost always together. How, in what possible way, can you be indebted to Mr. Crawford?"

Cecil had not the ready wit women are blessed with, and looked somewhat confused; an ill-natured person might have thought guilty.

" My dear Georgina," said Lady Helen, " I was in a difficulty—a serious difficulty, and this gentleman rescued me in the most generous manner."

" In a difficulty—what difficulty ?" asked Lady Georgina, much puzzled.

" I would tell you in a minute," said Helen, " for I was not the least to blame; but it would inculpate others, and I have promised not."

Lady Georgina was still more mystified. She could only suppose that some one had been rude or offended her sister, and Cecil had delivered her from them.

" But," she said," " surely they could not have known who you were."

" I believe," said Helen, demurely, " it was rather a case of mistaken identity."

" What ! were you taken for some one else ?" inquired Lady Georgina.

" I have vowed not to say a word,"

answered Lady Helen, " so do not tantalize
me. Some one was taken for some one
else, and I will not say another syllable,"
and she could not help laughing, though
she blushed violently.

" I think," said Cecil, " my reward is
greater than I deserve, and that you have
parted with what you value—I cannot
resign the pleasure altogether, but will
you exchange this for the least costly one
you possess, it will be exactly as valuable
to me."

And he took the diamond ring and
offered it to Helen, who shook her head
smiling.

" On the contrary," said Lady Georgina,
in her prettiest manner, " if you have
obliged my sister, you have obliged me;
you cannot refuse from me what you have
accepted from her."

And she took a beautiful sapphire pin
out of the shawl she wore, and held it to
him.

Cecil felt much embarrassed; he thought "Perhaps she wishes me to have it, that the gift of Lady Helen may not appear a peculiar favour," and in some measure it was her motive; Blanche too perceived it in a moment.

"Take it," she said to her brother, "Thank you, Lady Georgina, and let me assure you that my brother is the very reverse of a vain man. He deserves your good opinion far beyond what I can express. I must also mention that he would not tell me who it was who gave him the diamond ring, though he would not allow that it was a *gage d'amitié*."

"Pray consider it so from both of us," said Lady Georgina with her fascinating smile, "we are not going to remain here, still I trust our acquaintance will not terminate to-day."

"You are very good," said Blanche, "though I can hardly look forward to so much pleasure in our present circum-

stances. I can only repeat our hope that
you will remember your promise, and say
nothing of either of us, or of what has
taken place to-day."

" We promise," said the two," and they
parted, Lady Helen with the least possible
little sigh.

"He is much handsomer than young
Melford," she said to herself.

CHAPTER X.

THE next morning Mrs. Brewster
made some excuse to speak to
Blanche, who saw at once that the good
woman came charged up to the muzzle
with some wonderful news, which she was
dying to let off.

"Dear me, Miss! you must have heard
—all the country-side is ringing with it!"

"No, I have heard nothing," said
Blanche.

"Dear, dear! why I told you about Mr.
Joking Martinez! he's gone and done such
a wonderful thing! My Lady—his wife—
was run away with, all but down Langside
Grip; such a place you never see! and

Mr. Joking he rode up in such a way as never was—betwixt her and the Grip. The wonder was, and indeed a miracle, that they wasn't both hurled down and broke to bits—and the horses as well— and he saved her! Some folks do say he took a leap and jumped right across it; but that much I never will believe."

"And what did my Lady—his wife— say?"

"Oh! she fainted right off; and he carried her in his arms to the 'Red Rover' —a very bad place it is too; but there wasn't no other near, and there was my Lady Helen a-waiting for her, and thought she was dead; and she throwed herself o' top o' the dead body—-as she at least supposed it—and there was such a scene as would have drawed tears from a mile-stone."

"Well! and what else?"

"Oh! then Lady Helen, she fell on her knees before Mr. Joking and thanked him, and then she found her sister was not dead—and Mr. Joking, he sent for a carriage and four, and they all went off; and they do say that Mr. Joking is to be be made a Barrow-knight, 'cause of his bravery, only don't you think Miss as it'll sound queer—Sir Joking ?"

Blanche laughed heartily. She made no comment, but this history was a key to the diamond ring and the scene in the wood, and she understood it all, except the chief motive for preserving the secret, and allowing Martinez to have all the credit when he deserved none; but that it was in some way for the sake of the ladies, not of Sir Joking, as she ever after called him, she was certain; and thus ended the history of Mr. Martinez's exploit and of Lady Helen's diamond ring, for the secret was never disclosed; and Martinez was believed, for once in his life, to have done a brave thing.

CHAPTER XI.

BLANCHE, who now realized her ideas of cottage-life, in so far as she got up early in the morning to give Cecil his breakfast, was doing so when a packet of letters arrived through Mrs. Garratt. One was from Rosamond.

"Dear Cecil," she said, "I write to you because I fear that Blanche will not read my letters. Richard Conway and Mr. Henshawe both say that you have a right to all the valuables you possessed in the way of jewels and other things.

"There is a good deal here that belongs to you and your sister. She has left all her ornaments, some of them are of value. There are also many of your things.

" All that was given to you before our uncle's death is positively your own. I have collected them as far as I know, but I have very likely omitted some and locked them up safely until you tell me what you wish to be done. You promised to come to Crown-Harden. I wish you would soon, then you could make arrangements about your property that is here. My brother is going away in a week and will not return until April. The house is much less disagreeable during his absence. Blanche will not accept my love, but still I lay it at her feet. Dear Cecil, do come, I am not at all well."

He passed the letter in silence to Blanche, she coloured as she read it, but said not a word.

" I must get leave from Sir Philip Holland," said Cecil, after a pause.

"Then you mean to go ?" asked Blanche.

" Yes," said Cecil, " pray, dear Blanche, do not oppose it."

" Well, the jewels will be worth getting," she remarked, " I am glad they are our own. The best way will be to take what portion we wish to have sold, and leave the rest there. I do not think she will cheat us. I think they will be safe at Crown-Harden. I should be afraid of having things of value in this lonely place."

" I hope," said Cecil, " Sir Philip Holland will not object to giving me a short leave of absence. Barty Brewster will, I am sure, do everything right while I am away; and, Blanche, dear, you must have him and his wife in the house. I hope you will not feel nervous."

" I nervous ! what on earth should I be afraid of !" exclaimed Blanche, " that young demon, Stephen Granville, is not coming here, and he is the only dangerous person I know of."

" A boy of nineteen !" laughed Cecil.

" He is wicked enough for fifty," said
she. " He is more like a Malay than anything else—that Malay, in the papers the
other day, who struck a sailor on board-
ship as he hoped his deathblow, jumped
over-board, rose once, and with his head
just above the water cried out, ' Is he dead ?'
and sank down to rise no more. Stephen
Granville is just such another. A good
deal like Rosamond, but still more vindic-
tive. She is perhaps satisfied with having
ruined us—he would murder us too, if he
could."

" Nonsense," said Cecil.

" Truth," replied Blanche. " That
young viper is brimming over with venom,
towards you more especially; for every
thrashing you have given him he would
fain return a stab. I have seen his horrible
eyes glare at you."

" I wish I had acted differently in every
possible respect," said Cecil. " I was an

arrogant, domineering boy, and ungrateful to baseness towards Uncle Nicholas."

Blanche looked down and sighed, perhaps lately some such thoughts had presented themselves to her.

" Well," she said, after a pause, " it can't be helped. But, Cecil, grant me one request. In consideration of my forbearance in not saying one syllable to worry you about your going to Crown-Harden, against which I have the strongest possible prejudice, grant me this one request."

" I am sure I shall," was the answer " tell it me, Blanche."

" Promise me faithfully and solemnly," she said, " not to be in the house with Stephen Granville, no, not for one minute ; nor in the grounds, or any other place with him. Should he return unexpectedly, promise that you will leave at once and without delay."

" That is a promise I can easily give,"

said Cecil, " I have not the slightest desire
to be in his company."

" Then you promise ?" she asked.

" I do," he answered.

" Remember—you promise not to be in
the same house with him during your
absence, or to be in his company at all
while you are away."

" I promise," he said, smiling, " but,
Blanche, pray do not be so very tragic or
earnest, or I shall begin to imagine that
this lonely place affects your spirits."

" Not a bit," she answered, " I like it,
and as to old Barty Brewster, I have quite
a friendship for him—he is an amusing old
fellow. What kind of man is Sir Philip
Holland ?"

" Rather disagreeable," answered Cecil,
" have not you seen him ? he rides a stout
grey cob, and looks like a farmer—in his
dress at least. His face and features are
rather aristocratic, not quite unlike Lady
Dornington's, but less pleasant."

" Then they must be unpleasant indeed," said Blanche, who did not at all like Lady Dornington.

" I hope he will not call here while I am away," said Cecil, " if he does you had better not see him, he is very prying and inquisitive."

" What an odious man !" cried Blanche, " I hate him already !"

" Still," said Cecil, " it is convenient to be here for a time. In the Summer you will find it more cheerful. Spring is coming on, and these woods will be pretty then."

" Oh, yes," answered Blanche, " I hope we shall stay, I am ready to remain as long as you like. But one thing I beg. Do not inform Miss Rosamond where we are, or what we are doing, and tell her I am most especially merry and happy."

" Yes, dear," said Cecil, kindly, " I only hope it is true. This is a dull, lonely life for you, dear girl."

" Oh ! something will happen soon,"

Blanche replied, " we shall not be here all our lives."

" If you do not feel perfectly safe while I am absent," rejoined Cecil, " there is Mrs. Brewster's brother, let him sleep in the house too. I shall only be away three days, four at the utmost."

" Why you are grown quite an old woman, Cecil, what can happen to me? Absurd !"

" If I can," said Cecil, " I will just see Villeroy, he may be in town, or he may be at Deerham."

" Yes," Blanche answered, " but mind, he is not to come here, or know where we are, or I shall never forgive you. If you like, you may tell him I do not choose him to know; then if he has the impertinence to imagine that I admire him, he will be undeceived. He is a most horrid coxcomb."

" You never were so unjust in your life, Blanche, you do not know or understand him. He is the very reverse of a coxcomb

—only too modest, and the most generous, warm-hearted, good-natured fellow in the world."

" I hate good-natured fellows," said Blanche. " I never knew a man yet who could praise another man for anything in the world but good-nature. I rather dislike that excessive good-nature ! What I should admire would be striking talents, an ambitious, rising man."

" Rising ! I do not see that either of us is rising," said Cecil rather dolefully, in a tone that set Blanche off laughing.

" We still shall one day, I predict," she said, " trust me, Cecil, you will not end your days here as a game-keeper, or I in a cottage; of that I am absolutely certain."

" You are too confident," objected Cecil, " you make one almost afraid."

" Who's afraid ?" laughed Blanche proudly. " Not I—I defy fate, and the devil and all his works."

The following morning Cecil put on his

most orthodox attire, and called on Sir Philip Holland, who was by no means pleased to have a holiday asked for so soon.

"I know it is too soon," said Cecil, "and I would not ask it, except for very urgent business."

"And what very urgent business can a young man like you have?" sneered Sir Philip. "I cannot spare you."

Cecil hardly knew how to conceal his vexation.

"I thought," continued Sir Philip, "you told me you were not a married man."

"I am not," Cecil replied.

"Then who is the young woman at the forest lodge?" he inquired.

"My sister," was the answer.

"Your sister! Oh, indeed—your sister," said Sir Philip, with an unpleasant emphasis on the word.

"Yes, my sister," repeated Cecil, not quite in the tone of a dependent.

" That will do, Sir. You may go. I am engaged," said Sir Philip.

Cecil made his bow, and left him with more than ever of the angry soreness he always felt after speaking with Sir Philip Holland.

Though it was only March, there had been one or two fiercely hot days, and Cecil came into the cottage room hot and tired; throwing himself on a chair, he tossed his hat on to the table, and pushed back his wavy brown hair from his forehead. Blanche looked at him in admiration. Oddly enough, the gamekeeper's dress was very becoming to him; the long leather gaiters, generally so hideous, the red waistcoat and short coat, with his handsome discontented face, would have made a fortune on the stage.

"Has he refused?" asked Blanche, " Won't he let you go?"

"No," said Cecil. " It is not very pleasant, Blanche, to have a master."

"Oh! he'll change his mind," Blanche answered, " if you are very zealous and attentive, I dare say he will at last."

" I doubt it," said Cecil looking more melancholy than Blanche thought the occasion warranted.

"You have borne a great disappointment so well," said his sister, " do not grumble at a little one."

"It is not a little one to me," Cecil answered.

"I am sorry," Blanche rejoined seriously. " Well, if he won't let you. I will ask him myself."

"No, no, that will not do," Cecil replied.

" Well, have a cup of tea, and forget it," said Blanche, and as she passed him, she stooped down and gave him a kiss. He looked up in her face and smiled, all his ill-humour was dispersed.

CHAPTER XII.

MY dear Miss Rosamond, why won't you try to do as the doctor says ?" asked Mrs. Benson, as Rosamond sat leaning her elbow on her knee and her cheek on her hand. "Now if you could but do as Mr. Warren bids you, and just try a little horse exercise, what a thing it would be !"

"I can't; I'm not well enough," said Rosamond despondingly.

"But you might try, Miss Rosamond dear, I think you could."

"Mrs. Benson, why don't you go and pay a visit to the Queen of Golconda, it is not much further than the end of the world, and bring back your great, comfortable dimity pockets full of diamonds and rubies, and make Miss Blanche a rich lady again?"

"My dear, I can't, I wish I could."

"But you might try," said Rosamond.

"Ah, dear! well."

"No, do, dear Bunney, sit there, and make a comfortable lap," and Rosamond, curled up on the sofa like a little King Charles' spaniel, leant her head on the good soul's lap; it looked very uncomfortable, but Mrs. Benson stroked her hair and coaxed her, and Rosamond wanted to be petted, if by no one else, by Mrs. Benson.

"Do you feel very bad, my dear?"

"Yes, very," said Rosamond.

As she thus reposed, a letter was brought in, Rosamond took it languidly, without troubling herself to raise her head; for since she had been a great lady, letters poured in like a flood—circulars, notices from tradespeople, applications of every description—but she had scarcely caught sight of the writing of this one when she jumped up, and sat upright, pressing it between her two hands.

"Oh! Mrs. Benson, this is from Cecil and Blanche!" for she always coupled them in this manner, it being easier to her than to say Cecil alone.

"Well, my dear, why don't you open it?"

"Yes, I am going—what can it be?"

"Had not you better look, Miss Rosamond, dear?"

So adjured Rosamond did look, and sprang to her feet, her eyes sparkling, her cheek flushed.

"What is it, my dear?"

"He is coming—quite soon—perhaps in a fortnight. Oh! I thought I should never see them again."

"My dear!" expostulated Mrs. Benson.

"Let's go and see to his room, his

own room, Mrs. Benson, let us have it all comfortable."

"Time enough, my dear; and I'll engage I'll see to that; when it's set to rights you shall come and see whether it's all nice or not. I am pleased, my dear Miss Granville."

"Call me Miss Rosamond," she said, "only think, Mrs. Benson, suppose I were to surprise him—I do think he would be pleased—suppose I were to try to learn to ride, I really think he would like it. I was so stupid about it."

"Do, my dear," said Mrs. Benson, "why not now at once."

"I really will!" exclaimed Rosamond, forgetting her aching head and her weakness, she put on a hat and shawl, and ran down to the stables to Zuleika, who had been a pet ever since Cecil left Crown-Harden. She fondly patted her satin-like coat, kissed her velvet nose, then threw her arms round Zuleika's neck, and burst into hysterical tears; fortunately, ere long, she heard some of the grooms moving outside, when she checked herself, and took the first opportunity to fly upstairs and get ready.

Cecil, on the day that he had persuaded her to attempt horsemanship, had begged Mrs. Benson to send a note to his London tailor, and to order a handsome habit, hat, and all requisite ; and in paying his various bills, when last in town, had felt a little flush of pleasure in pulling out the rather heavy sum they had cost—decidedly the only payment he had to make that did occasion any such sensation.

Rosamond took out the habit, looked at it admiringly, and put it on—so good of him, she thought. She came down, and Zuleika was again at the front door; but this time it was only a groom who put her on. She was in such a state of excitement, she never even thought of fear, and at the proper time and place set off at a long

canter—Zuleika seeming to tread the air.
She experienced a new and exquisite sensation, the swift breeze meeting her brow, the
light, easy motion, the elastic swing of the
smooth canter, approaching to a gallop—a
sort of wild delight danced in her eyes
and sent the blood kindling to her heart.
She sat with a freedom and ease that
astonished the man, an elderly, respectable
groom, the same who had witnessed her
former ignominious failure.

"Why, Miss," he said, "you must have
been bewitched some time back; you ride
beautiful now."

Rosamond smiled. "Ah!" she thought,
"when Cecil comes this will be joy indeed;"
but, enchanting as it was, her strength
was small, and after a few miles, she most
unwillingly found herself obliged to turn
Zuleika's head homewards.

"I will ride as far as I can every day
till he comes, and I think he will say I am
improved."

She did not know why it would be so very delightful to her to be praised by Cecil. She fulfilled her intention, inquiring with the greatest earnestness of Thomas how she ought to sit, how to hold the bridle, how to start Zuleika off from one pace to another; and Thomas, who, respectable as he was, had felt some slight contempt for her ever since her first deplorable exhibition on Zuleika, began to regard her with respect.

" I allus say," he declared, " that them as isn't no ways fond of the 'osses, can't have much in 'em—surely no good—there's summat wrong at bottom. You mark my words, Sandy, for I've had some experience in life, he or she either as sits a horse like a sack, and nothing else, and handles 'em like a coal-heaver, sich-like ain't fit not to walk this blessed earth, and it's me as says it."

" Ay, Thomas," Sandy would respond; " men may be good sometimes; women not so often; but the 'osses, they always is; and if anybody says the contrary, why I'll punch their heads for 'em."

"The boy's beyond his years," said Thomas approvingly, and Sandy quite coincided in the opinion.

But Rosamond's state of rapture could not last, and Mrs. Benson was sorry to see her again pale and melancholy.

"Why, you don't seem so happy now, Miss Rosamond?"

"No."

"But why not?"

"Mrs. Benson, I'm sure he won't come."

"But he said he would—I'm sure he will, Miss Rosamond. Why shouldn't he?"

"Miss Blanche will not like him to come, and he would never do what would vex her."

"Oh! he'll come, Miss Rosamond, I'm quite sure."

"He may not like to leave his sister alone; he would have written again to mention the day."

"Why do you take such pleasure in making yourself unhappy, Miss Rosamond? he's as like to come as not."

"As like to come as not!" repeated Rosamond, indignantly; "and just now you said you were sure he would come."

"Well, you know, we can't be sure of anything. I am no prophet, only I think he will; but indeed, Miss Rosamond, you shouldn't give way so—it is not right."

"I know it is not, dear Mrs. Benson. I intend to try to overcome it; but I feel a weight like lead. Still, I know it is wrong."

"And don't you know how you used to say if you could but be let alone, and do a little how you liked, you asked for nothing more; and yet now see you're worse than ever."

"Yes," said Rosamond; "but do not

desert me. You are the only person in the world who cares for me."

"How could I, my dear? You're made to be loved, and you will be one of these days."

It was a homely and odd sort of consolation, and it made Rosamond smile. Yet in good truth it came near to touch the secret malady of her heart.

CHAPTER XIII

BARTY BREWSTER had very soon granted his full measure of approbation to Cecil Conway—whom, however, he did not know by that name, but as Charles Crawford, the one he had chosen as having the same initials as his own.

It was rather magnanimous on the part of Barty, as he had much wished to obtain the situation for himself, being quite capable of undertaking it; but he bore his rival no grudge, on the contrary he exerted himself to assist him, and give him all the information he could.

"There's one man," he said, confidentially, "I hope you won't come across—

he's a confirmed poacher, but if you're
wise you'll keep out of his way. It's Black
Ben—or as we call him now, Big Ben—it's
my notion that the great Parliament bell
was christened after him. He's the worst
poacher in the country. He can't abide a
gamekeeper, and will fight 'em when he
gets a chance. He's an ugly customer, he
is, poor chap!"

"Why do you call him poor?" asked
Cecil.

"Well, I don't know. He's a widower,
and he's very fond of his little gal. He
wanted to marry our Betsy that's out in
service, but she wouldn't have nothing to
say to him—he wasn't steady enough. Yet
if he hadn't such a bad character about
here, and could get work, I don't know
but what he'd be different. He's one that
must be always in extremes, you know."

Not long after, Cecil had a chance of
seeing this formidable personage. He was
above six feet high, broad-shouldered,

deep-chested, well-made, with a bushy
black beard, whiskers and eyebrows. He
gave Cecil a bold fierce stare as he passed
him that promised no amity; and to tell
the truth, Cecil did not feel an ardent
desire for a more intimate acquaintance.
Indeed for some time it seemed not likely
to come to pass, nor did he much wish
Blanche to see his formidable, broad-
shouldered enemy. But one sunny afternoon as they were returning together from
Church, loitering along the hedge-side of
a pleasant field, they suddenly came upon
him as he lay basking in the sun, enjoying
himself in his own lazy fashion, stretched
full length on his back, with his head resting on his two up-raised arms, and his old
felt hat pulled low to shade his eyes. He
did not condescend to alter his rough
every-day attire for the Sunday, as a mark
of scorn for all established and respectable
customs. Before they quite came up to
him a little girl, who was gathering a few

early daisies, ran right in front of Blanche, at the risk of tripping her up, and staring earnestly in her face, gave two or three short rustic curtseys, after the manner of village children. But this was no common village child. Her complexion had a rich, warm tint in it that was a beauty in itself; her vermillion lips, and the bright damask flush on her cheek, suited well with a pair of large black eyes that fixed at once the attention of Blanche. They, as well as the rest of her countenance were brilliant, not with the mere mirth of childhood, but with a strange, almost solemn light. So earnest was the little girl's gaze that Blanche had time to return it, and stoop down to kiss her. She had scarcely done so, when the tall fellow lounging near sprang to his full height, and in a most uncivil manner snatched the child's hand and drew her away.

"A surly ruffian!" exclaimed Cecil angrily in his hearing.

The man turned a silent scowl on him, unseen by Blanche, and walked leisurely on in the opposite direction.

" Who is it ?" inquired Blanche.

" A fellow they call Ben Darley," replied her brother.

" What is he ?" she asked ; " a poacher, I am certain."

" Yes, they say so," answered Cecil carelessly.

" Oh, Cecil," she exclaimed, " have nothing to do with him."

" No," said Cecil, " I do not intend ; he looks more like a Neapolitan bandit than an Englishman."

" Yes," observed Blanche, " he would make a good picture ; but what a lovely child !"

" Yes, I think her pretty, but all children are alike," said Cecil, who did not possess a very lively appreciation of small children.

" My dear Cecil! where are your eyes ? I never saw one to approach her."

" I only saw that she nearly threw you down, bobbing in your path, just under your feet," Cecil replied.

" Well, never mind," exclaimed Blanche ; " but you have a great deal to learn."

On a fine frosty morning, a day or two afterwards, as Cecil was quietly pacing down one of the alleys in the wood, with his gun on his shoulder, Blanche came running after him as light as a lapwing, and sprang on him with her arms round his neck, and a merry burst of gleeful laughter.

" What has brought you here ?" exclaimed Cecil.

" Oh !" said Blanche, still out of breath, " I was standing at the window, indulging in a ' sollyquolly,' as Mary Villeroy used to call it, when what should I see but an old grey cart-horse jogging along with an ugly monster of a man on the top of it, so I

was sure it must be the Ogre of the Abbey,
and off I ran into the woods after you,
and turned down this way, and that
way, and the other way, and I was so
pleased to see you plodding along like
an old man of eighty; here, sit by me,"
and she dropped down on a fallen log, " or
no, go and get me some blackberries."

" Blackberries, child! why, the black-
thorn is scarce out yet!"

" Never mind, dear patriarchal grand-
father, sit by me and—look here!"

So saying, she pulled three large pears
out of her little apron-pocket triumphantly,
" that dear, darling old Brewster sent them
to me; they are so delicious. I was so
greedy as to eat one."

Thus chatting, she ate her pear, then
jumped up.

" Come on," she exclaimed, " I will
make the rounds with you," and passing
her arm through Cecil's, walked on with
him, little guessing that a pair of keen

grey eyes, assisted by an eye-glass and a pair of sharp ears appertaining to them, had seen and listened to all her careless words.

" So !" said Sir Philip Holland, crashing through the bushes, " an ugly old monster, the Ogre of the Abbey ! Thank you, young lady—a little vixen, I must see more of her and teach her better—so those old Jezebels are right after all—more pretty than proper, decidedly, and more pretty than fraternal. *I* do not jump into Lady Dornington's arms in that *effrenée* manner. A merry little devil, too ! I think I shall go and give her a lecture to-morrow."

But even Sir Philip Holland, autocrat as he was, could not always do as he wished ; on the morrow he was laid up with a severe fit of gout, and his temper, not at the best the most serene, was so savage at such times that every one kept out of his way as much as possible, knowing that he was, fortunately for them, not in a condition to come to them. All avoided him except his housekeeper, Mrs. Arnicott, who at such times did not neglect to strengthen her authority and influence, and sought to amuse him by collecting and retailing to him all the small scandals of the neighbourhood.

She was sufficiently cunning to perceive that any little details regarding the young lady at the gamekeeper's cottage entertained her master, but was unable to discover whether it pleased him better to hear good or ill of her. Unfortunately there was no good known to record, but a good deal of ill to suspect, and the latter is the more fruitful source of conversation; besides that, Mrs. Arnicott had herself conceived a bad opinion of the flighty young person as she denominated her. To be pretty and merry, and care for nobody, was not the way to gain the good graces of a staid middle-aged lady with strong prejudices and narrow experience, though the mere circumstance of having lived the greater portion of her life in seclusion at Holland Abbey gave her an idea that her own wisdom was unerring.

CHAPTER XIV.

WHAT was most unpleasant to Cecil, was when now and then Sir Philip had a shooting party, and he, as well as the under-gamekeeper, was expected to attend. Hitherto he had been so fortunate as to escape meeting any former acquaintances of his own, for he was not philosopher enough to regard such a chance with unconcern.

The shooting season was now past, but one morning he was summoned to attend an otter-hunting party that was to start from the Abbey, and proceed to a stream at some considerable distance across the country.

There were a good many gentlemen assembled about the gates of the pleasure gardens waiting for Sir Philip Holland, mostly on horseback, and among them Cecil started at recognizing Stephen Granville, who had procured, through Lady Dornington, an invitation for a few days at Holland Abbey.

Stephen also was struck with amazement on discovering Cecil. He stared at him long and insolently, and gave a sneering laugh; both young men happened to be rather in the back ground, therefore Stephen resolved not to lose his opportunity, pushed his horse rudely against Cecil.

" Get out of the way, can't you?" he exclaimed, pretending not to have been able to avoid him.

There was still some delay as to which way they would take, no one seemed to pay much attention to Granville who was in a desperate ill-humour, considering himself neglected. He dropped his whip, whether accidentally or not it was hard to say.

" Pick up my whip," he exclaimed, in his most bullying tone.

Cecil coloured deeply; his anger began to burn hot within him, but he commanded himself and did it without a remark, supposing that in accordance with his present situation he ought to do so, and being moreover anxious to avoid any *éclat* or explanation, for he had no wish to appear under the character of a poor gentleman in difficulties. One or two of the gentlemen had noticed Granville's offensive manner, and were pleased with Conway's behaviour and appearance.

" It looks like a premeditated thing," said one.

" Bad style of man," remarked another.

Granville's insolence and aversion were inflamed, rather than soothed by Cecil's forbearance. He observed his cousin's reluctance to betray his real position, and meanly resolved to make every use of his advantage over him. In the same authoritative style as before, he ordered him to open a side-gate leading by a back-way to the stables. It had been rainy in the night, and this road being seldom used, was deep in mud.

Cecil paused, for it was ankle deep; Granville gave his horse a fierce tug, and made him caper so as intentionally to splash the mire upon Cecil.

On this Cecil determined to bear no more, turned his back on Granville, and returned to the place where he had been at first.

" Did you hear me, rascal ?" said Granville furiously, and spurring his horse in front of Cecil, struck him across the face with his whip ; at so outrageous an insult all Cecil's prudence forsook him, he sprang forward, seized Granville by the front of his coat, and dragging him off his horse, flung him on his back in the mud, with one knee on his chest, and one hand on his throat, rapid as lightning.

Stephen felt his grasp like an iron collar tightening round his throat, half stifled he only spoke one word, " Rosamond !"

Cecil's eyes were flashing, the veins of his forehead stood up like whip-cord ; but at that word he relaxed his hold, sprang to his feet, and in an instant lifted Granville upright by the arm.

" Get up—I won't hurt you, Stephen," and forgetting all present, he turned to leave the place.

As he passed Sir Philip Holland, who had made his appearance some minutes before, he for the first time recollected himself.

" Excuse me for to-day, Sir Philip," he said.

" Go home, boy, go straight home," was the answer.

Granville also turned back into the

house, livid with disappointed rage, and swearing revenge.

"Served the fellow right," said one of the gentlemen to Sir Philip. "I saw it all, it was a regular persecution."

"Very impudent to a servant of mine," said Sir Philip, who had been much disposed to do the very thing Cecil had done. They all rode off, while Cecil scarcely knew which way to take.

He felt ashamed to display to Blanche the tell-tale red mark across his face, and was still more unwilling to relate to her his encounter with Stephen Granville, particularly after the anxious caution she had so lately given him. He wandered therefore to some distant coverts, and did not return to his cottage till late, when he knew that Blanche, who had been unwell, would be gone upstairs.

That night Cecil had not been long in bed when he heard shots fired in the wood. Of course he jumped up, dressed, and prepared to go out. As he passed Blanche's door, she came out to him in her white dressing-gown, with a face almost as white.

"Oh, Cecil! don't go out to-night, pray don't," she said, shivering.

"My darling Blanche, you would not not have me such a craven—of course I must. Why I shall be back in an hour."

"No, no, those guns! I am afraid," she whispered.

"Nonsense, child," said Cecil, "it's only the game they're after—they won't take me for a hare."

"Ah! but I know well the danger, you cannot deceive me."

"Danger! there's none, or very little ; but you cannot expect me to stand by, and let them range about unmolested," said he.

"Then get Brewster to go with you, do dear Cecil."

"It would be no use my going at all

if I went round to the village first, and
had to wait for old Brewster. Don't be
afraid, I'll take care of myself; I have a
very salutary regard for my own safety."

"Oh! I shall be wretched till you come
back," exclaimed Blanche.

"Pray don't be so, darling; but they'll
be all off before I get there."

"I wish they may," she ejaculated, as
he ran down-stairs, and went out, locking
the door after him.

Poor Blanche, who had been unwell the
day before, sat trembling, and shivering,
opening the window every few minutes to
listen; at last she heard the loud report
of a gun, and an agony like that of death
ran cold through her veins.

"Oh Heaven! pity him and me!" she
exclaimed. And every fault and error of
her life stood threatening before her fancy.
"If something dreadful happens, I deserve it all; but oh, in mercy, still spare
us!" And as she looked round in her

great fear, she could have believed she saw the deathly face of Uncle Nicholas lying there on her pillow.

She could have screamed; but if she had, she knew she should lose all self-control, and she restrained herself. "Oh!" she thought, "if she—if he could live over those last months once more, how different she would be! How kind! how attentive!"

She again opened her casement and leant out. It was so very still, even the stars looked dim and faint; the long range of dark woodland gave no voice, there was not a sound to be heard, but the air was soft and cooled her throbbing temples.

But it is time to return to Cecil Conway, who, following the direction of the sound he had heard, soon found himself in one of the broad ridings of the forest.

It was a dull night, quite dark under the shade of the trees, but objects could be dimly seen in the open. He soon discerned two figures, looking black and burly in the indistinct, pale star-light. One was a big tall man, the other much less.

Without a moment's hesitation he advanced, and laid his hand on the collar of the big man, who tried to shake him off; but Cecil was as resolved as he, and they were soon struggling fiercely.

His antagonist had the advantage in strength and size, but Cecil had skill, and was also strong and active, and much quicker than his opponent. They had exchanged some hard blows before the shorter man interfered, and when he did, it was not so much to take an active part in the battle as to embarrass Cecil. Once he thrust a stick between his legs with the intention of throwing him down, and nearly succeeded ; but Cecil gave him a back-hander and sent him reeling. He was now beginning to feel that he should not be able to hold out much longer; just then the shorter ruffian returned upon him, grinding his teeth, infuriated beyond control.

"Stephen Granville," exclaimed Cecil imprudently, "I know you."

"—— him, cut his throat," he heard in a hissing whisper that seemed close to his very ears, and he caught sight of the gleam of a knife-blade. It was life for life. Collecting all his strength, he dealt the big fellow a blow just behind his ear, and he went down like a stone; at the same instant he shoved with his shoulder, and with his whole force, the second ruffian, who, taken by surprise, staggered backwards. Before he could recover himself, Cecil was upon him, wrenched the knife from his grasp, and flung it as far as he could into the wood—then glancing at the burly figure stretched on the ground stunned and motionless, he felt it unnecessary to wait till he should recover, perhaps to attack him again, and turning from the scene of the conflict, he walked leisurely home.

Before he had gone a hundred yards a pistol shot was fired after him, and the shot rattled among the leaves and twigs above his head.

" Treacherous villain !" he said, and proceeding beneath the shady side, he turned down one of the many narrow alleys that branched off from the main riding and reached his home safely, but so exhausted and faint that he could only un-dress and throw himself into bed. As he passed his sister's door softly, not to dis-turb her, she called :

" Cecil, dear, are you safe ?"

" Yes, quite ; all right. Go to sleep, dear Blanche," he answered.

CHAPTER XV.

CECIL awoke early the next morning somewhat refreshed, but very stiff, with an aching head, a black eye, and a sprained wrist, luckily the left.

All that had taken place came vividly before his remembrance. What would Sir Philip say to the *fracas* of the preceding day, and how should he act with regard to the scene at night? Believing the actors in it to be poachers, Sir Philip would expect to hear all particulars, but could he reveal the conduct of Stephen Granville? Ruffianly as it had been, he felt it an impossibility to expose him; he was Rosamond's brother—Rosamond! and at that

name a warm glow, delicious and new to
him, pervaded his whole being. Rosamond! his cousin, his love—yes, he knew
it now—dear Rosamond! sweet, gentle,
generous; a fresh heaven appeared to
open before him, and her soft eyes seemed
to smile on him.

The first emotion of this new conscious-
ness was rapture, but not for long; no, he
might slave, he might die for her, but he
could never win her. They were parted,
there was no hope, and he had never
known her value till too late; but still he
would suffer all things rather than grieve
her; yes, for Stephen there was full im-
punity, let him do what he could.

He arose with a heavy heart, and went
out quietly, not to disturb his sister; as
soon as he got outside his door, he received
a message from Sir Philip, saying he
wished to speak with him at once.

"I suppose," thought Cecil, "he is

going to dismiss me, what will become of us next?"

Early as it was, Sir Philip had breakfasted, and Granville also; the latter was sitting in the study with Sir Philip.

He had spent a night of misery; cowed, terrified, aghast at his own wickedness, he dreaded exposure, feeling that he was very near to being a murderer. The brand of Cain had seared, if it had not stamped him. Yet it was no repentance that he felt; his hatred was more suppressed, but deeper than ever.

When Cecil entered, Sir Philip was writing, and Stephen Granville was leaning back in an arm-chair, his arms a kimbo, his hands on his two sides, his legs stretched out as far as they would go. He gave one evil, downcast look at Cecil, then turned away; and Cecil, as he stood there, tall, upright, and frank, felt that his enemy was subdued, if not conquered.

Granville was cadaverously pale, and the mingled gloom, shame, and fierceness on his face gave Cecil an impression of something almost like pity.

"So, Sir," said Sir Philip, looking up at last, "you're here, are you?"

Cecil bowed.

"I allow of no fighting in my presence, nobody is permitted to play the bully here except myself. A person in your humble situation must learn to submit. If a gentleman does you some little injustice you must bear it. Do you hear, Sir?"

"I do," said Cecil.

"If this happens again, I send you off at a day's notice. And you, Sir," he added, turning to Granville, "when you ill-use my servant, it is a liberty, and an offence to me. Wait a moment, please, I wish to hear what took place last night. I heard shots. There were poachers about. You've had another fight," he said, looking at Cecil.

" Yes," answered Cecil, " I went out to them."

" What did you do, Sir ?"

" I knocked one of them down, and went home again."

" How many were there ?"

" Two."

" Why did you not take their guns, pray ?"

" They had no guns," said Cecil.

" No guns! What were the shots? No guns !"

" It was a pistol," said Cecil.

" A pistol! Pshaw! don't tell me ! who were they ?"

" It was very dark," Cecil replied.

" Was one of them that scoundrel Big Ben ?"

" It was too dark to swear to him."

" You know well enough !" said Sir Philip impatiently, " what motive have you for screening him I should like to know? Who was the other? What was he like?"

"He was shorter," said Cecil.

"As tall as this gentleman? Will you do me the favour to stand up, Mr. Granville."

Stephen hesitated, but to refuse would not look well, he stood up accordingly; but so mean, so abject, so shrunken did he appear by the side of Cecil that Sir Philip laughed.

"Was he as tall as this gentleman?" he repeated.

"It was too dark to see," said Cecil again quietly.

"Well," said Sir Philip, "you have knocked down Big Ben—here's a slight reward. If you apprehend him, it shall be five."

And he threw down two sovereigns on the table before Cecil.

"Thank you, Sir Philip," he said, "but I cannot take them. It was in self-defence, not in your service."

" Oh, well ! if you like, I like it quite as well," said Sir Philip, hastily pocketing again his gift. " Now, young man, mind what you're about, or you'll get into a worse scrape than this. You ought to beg this gentleman's pardon."

Cecil looked full at Stephen for the first time and smiled.

" Both were to blame," he said, " I bear no ill-will."

Stephen grunted something inarticulate, and went out. Cecil was about to follow, when Sir Philip called out :

" Here, you Crawford, come back ! I have some recollection of your asking for a holiday, have I not ?"

" Yes, Sir," said Cecil, with a beating at his heart.

" Well, you may have it, but only for a week mind you."

" Oh, thank you, Sir Philip !" exclaimed Cecil, with a little more animation than was necessary.

Sir Philip bent a curious, inquisitive glance on him, and Cecil made his bow and retired, far more happy than Stephen Granville.

The latter could not shake off a sense of discomfiture and of guilt. His feelings were not much more evil than they had been; but they had borne fruit, and the taste even to him was bitter.

He dreaded lest his deeds of the night should be exposed; he was somewhat startled to find to what lengths his malevolent temper had nearly hurried him. On undertaking this act of revenge, he had, as he thought, guarded against any fatal results, by forbidding Ben to carry his gun—he himself only putting his pistol in his pocket for the purpose of luring Cecil out by firing it. He had hoped for an easy victory when he looked at the limbs and muscles of his ally, who had declared that he always thought it a good job to give a game-keeper a beating. He was enraged at the strong resistance made by Cecil, he expected to see him conquered and battered—he would not have cared if he were injured. He smiled as he pictured to himself his haughty young cousin beaten down to the ground, bruised and wounded, limping off, perhaps, with a broken limb ; but he had not contemplated death.

When he heard his own name, when he knew himself to be recognized and exposed, a savage impulse he could not command prompted him to silence his enemy for ever. The strife, the excitement had kindled the fiery demon within him, and he was alarmed at the spirit he had evoked. The gleam of the knife haunted his fancy, death seemed standing by his side, and added to all was the dread of being denounced.

On hearing that Sir Philip had sent for Cecil, an uneasy craving, yet shrinking from hearing what would be said, overcame him; he determined to be present, and know the worst. Should he be accused, would a sturdy denial serve him? it could be but one man's word against another's— nothing could be proved. When Cecil generously spared him he felt no gratitude, Cecil had gained one more advantage over him, that was all. He still stood high and noble above him, lowered in station as he was.

He left that day without a civil word from Sir Philip Holland, who merely nodded a slighting adieu, without even offering his hand. Stephen had turned away to go, when he resolved to leave, if he could, a sting behind him; he stopped, and addressing Sir Philip said:

"I will give you one caution, at any rate—be on your guard against that fellow who acts as your gamekeeper. I know more of him than you do. He is not the honest fellow he seems. You are deceived in him, and duped, and so you will find some day. · I happen to know him. I am sorry to see you so taken in. Good morning."

On leaving home Stephen's friend, Orlando Henshawe, had been absent on business, and on his return he took good care not to impart to him a syllable of what had occurred. Even apart from the unfortunate events of the night, he never intended to inform his friend where Cecil was. There was a large amount of secretiveness in his temper; besides, he had often felt a jealous displeasure at Henshawe's superior knowledge in matters of law, and his general knowingness, if such a word may be employed; and by having information that Henshawe had not, Granville hoped, as he expressed it, to take a rise out of him.

When Cecil returned home from Sir Philip Holland's about dinner-time, Blanche was greatly disturbed on seeing him.

"Oh, Cecil," she cried, "how those brutes have knocked you about! How cruel! How was it?"

"There was nothing to tell," Cecil answered; "but the row was a lucky one for me. On the strength of it, I suppose, Sir Philip has given me my leave of absence."

"Has he?" exclaimed Blanche, half pleased, half regretfully.

"But I shall not go till you are quite well again, Blanche," said Cecil.

"Oh, I am well enough," she replied.

"I must wait till I have got rid of these ornaments. They look rather disreputable," said Cecil.

CHAPTER XVI.

SHORTLY after Cecil's night adventure, as he was returning from the village one day, he happened to meet Big Ben.

The man as he passed, looked earnestly at him out of the corner of his eye from beneath his bushy black eyebrows, and to the surprise of Cecil touched his cap—a piece of civility that he never vouchsafed to Sir Philip Holland, or anyone. Cecil looked after him. He felt a young man's admiration for the strength and physical power of the giant's frame; and he fancied there was something he liked in the fellow's rough but manly features.

So much so that he determined to pay him a visit; and on the first opportunity he did so.

His hut was built on a piece of waste land, a little removed from the high road. On Cecil knocking at the door, its owner made his appearance, with a little bright-eyed, fearless-looking girl perched on his shoulder, like a little bird, she sat so lightly and so firmly.

Ben removed her, and with the utmost care deposited her on the ground in some confusion; but his innate feeling of hospitality overcame it, and he immediately invited Cecil to come in.

"Come in—pray step in, Sir, won't you?" he said, with an attempt at courtesy.

Cecil followed. His home was little better than a hovel. There was not much furniture in it; but what there was was tidy, and neatly arranged. The only decent articles were a small child's chair and table, and a low shelf of her own height, on which were ranged some playthings of rough home construction.

He gave Cecil a chair, and sat down, the child clasping his knee, and gazing with bold, wide-open eyes at Cecil. Ben bent down his head to her, and lifted her up on his lap.

"I have had a mind to speak to you some time," said Ben.

"Then I am glad I happened to call on you," Cecil replied.

"Well, Sir, you might have done me a damage, and you did not. I mean you might have had me up. I should not have cared except for the child. I wanted to say a word or two about that night."

"I had rather not hear anything about it," said Cecil, "I always let bygones be bygones. But yours is a bad trade, why don't you leave it?"

"Sometimes I wish I could," was the answer, "but you know in these parts I've not got a good character. 'Give a dog a bad name and hang him,' as folks say. I can't get work. Our Squire is set against me, with some cause, I don't deny."

"I wonder you don't emigrate," said Cecil, "you are a fellow who would get on well in Australia, and soon come back a rich man."

"I've often thought of it," said Ben, "and would to-morrow but for the child— the child you see—when my poor girl died her last words were, 'be good to the child, Ben,' and I have been good to her any way, and what's more, it's the only thing alive I love."

The child understood him, and stroked his thick black beard fondly. Poor as she was, in one heart, at least, she was a little queen.

"She is a pretty child!" said Cecil, admiringly.

This won Ben's heart at once.

"She is, Sir, and has got more sense than I have, little as she looks. I hate the mines, but I have thought of that; then again I should have to leave her alone all day. If she had a good-tempered mother to look after her it might do, but no good girl would have a word to say to me. I liked Betsy Brewster well enough."

"When your child grows up to be a handsome, honest girl, you would not like to see her ashamed of you," remarked Cecil.

This was a new idea for Ben; he stopped short, he had never thought of his little Jessy but as the tiny idol she was now.

"You've got some money, I suppose," said Cecil, " to go on with for a time?"

Ben's brown face reddened.

"I have a bit of money I never liked so little, but"——

"Then," interrupted Cecil, "go on steadily for a time, get into no mischief, keep quiet, go to church"——

"Church!" exclaimed Ben, " that's no go, I've not been since"——

" The more reason for going now, but I make no conditions, I only wish you would," said Cecil. " If you go on well for a few months I may be able to be of use to you. I am almost as poor as yourself, but I have a friend who might help you."

" The people about here do whisper that you're a gentleman, but now I know it," burst out Ben, gratefully. " Oh, Mr. Crawford, you must let me say a word or two that is heavy on my mind. That night, Sir, I never did such a thing before. I've had many a tussle, but never before for pay; I did not like it, I tell you, Sir, but I wanted the gold, and the gentleman, he said, he meant no serious harm by you, only to get you a sound thrashing; and, says he, it'll serve you right, for you were a sneaking rascal, and thinks I that's what every game-keeper deserves, a plague on 'em. And I think you'd ha' got off worse than you did, only just before you fetched me a thump on the ear, I caught a sight of the knife, and it took me aback as it were—for that's what I never used, and never would. The varmint had told me he never wanted to come nigh murder."

" Nor did he, I am sure," said Cecil, " it was an unpremeditated impulse, and I believe it annoys him as much as anyone. I forgive him, and wish he felt no worse towards me than I do towards him."

Ben stared; he was not sure whether he admired such sentiments or not, but, at all events, he liked the man.

"Well," he said, after some thought, " you're a good friend, though not much of a hater. I used to think who loves well, must hate well too; but if ever you want a strong man to stand by you, think of me, I'll never fail you—try me else."

" I believe you," said Cecil, heartily.

" And," added Ben, " if that chap as called you a sneaking cur, which he is himself, should come alongside again, I'll give him what he wanted me to give you and welcome."

" No, thank you," said Cecil.

" But the art and cunning of the man !" exclaimed Ben. " He says to me, ' take no gun with you, mind, and there'll be no mischief;' and when we were at the place, out he pulls his pistol from his pocket, and says he, ' that's the pretty little call-bird that'll decoy him, for, mind you, we are to be poachers, we are '—and then he fires it off two or three times for you to hear. And says he to spite me up, ' you're not afraid I hope, Ben, he's an active young fellow ; but you must give it him well, don't spare him, he's as tough as a horse ; cuff him and kick him till he begs for mercy,' and says I, ' leave that to me,' for I'd heard you were as strict over the preserves as Sir Philip himself, and was ravening against all of us."

" So far I am," said Cecil, " that if you were poaching, and I came upon you, I

would do my best against you, don't you
see it's my duty ? it's what a game-keeper
is paid for."

" Then why are you a game-keeper?"
asked Ben, reproachfully.

" Ah ! that's a long question to answer.
But if the game is Sir Philip's, he has a
right to keep it, and defend it too."

" Well," said Ben, frowning, " that's
neither here nor there. But all the same,
I'll never be less your friend, and I only
wish I could serve you."

At parting they shook hands with great
cordiality, and before Cecil left, Ben put
the child's face towards Cecil, and as she
deposited a little cool, moist kiss on his
cheek, the poor fellow really believed he
had given some reward to his generous
friend, while Cecil after he had left the
place, laughed a little to himself, it being
evident Ben deemed it a favour; but Cecil
had not been accustomed to babies, nor
did he prize much their kisses.

CHAPTER XVII.

ONE day Mrs. Brewster came to the Lodge, bringing with her little Jessie Darley, carrying a bunch of early primroses and snow-drops, with Ben Darley's duty to the young lady. The little girl held out her nosegay, looking up in evident admiration at Blanche, whose beauty seemed to make a lasting impression on this little child of nature.

Blanche thanked and kissed her, and put her on her lap, where the little girl sat silent, drooping her pretty face in overpowering shyness.

" Now that's a queer thing," observed Mrs. Brewster, " that Jessie should be bashful with you, Miss ; why she's as free and fearless as a little sparrow, she is mostly—it ain't because she does not like you, Miss, for she's been a-chattering away all the time about you."

"Do you like me, darling?" asked Blanche.

Jessie slowly raised her long, black lashes, and gazed in her face a moment with a whispered, "Yes."

If Jessie admired Blanche, the feeling was reciprocal. The little girl's features were but softly defined, as those of a child should be, but there was no irregularity in the sweet, pure, full oval of the little countenance. The small nose was straight, the round dewy lips were beautifully moulded, the colour on her cheeks, though rich, was transparent, such as is seldom seen in a brunette except among the rare beauties of the South, the hue, though brilliant, was tender, the black hair soft as silk, the black eyes large and melting, yet withal Blanche could see the strongest likeness to her father, though embellished and refined—there was the touch of wildness, too, that is seen in creatures of the forest.

" Surely," thought Blanche, " this little child, if she lives, will be a genius."

Partly to test this fancy of hers she brought her a book of pictures, some very good ones; the child's attention was arrested at once, and as she became interested her shyness wore off; one of them especially attracted her; it was from a well-known picture of angels carrying a dead girl with long fair hair through a starry night sky. She turned to this again and again; then she suddenly looked up at Blanche. It was clear that she thought there was a resemblance between Blanche and that fair, lifeless girl; a sadness came over her dear little face, and Blanche managed to put the book away and find something else to amuse her.

This visit was so pleasant to both the child and the young girl that it was arranged that Jessie should come and spend the Sunday with Blanche. Ben was going some distance to see a relation of his who was well off, hoping he might get him some employment, for he came of people in a respectable class of life and had had a tolerable education.

The little girl came to the Lodge after church, holding Sally Brewster's hand very tight; but Blanche, whose nature it was to charm man, woman and child, soon made her even more than before feel happy and at her ease.

She read to her some simple but well-written stories, and was glad to find that Jessie was not ignorant, and understood them well. Ben, though careless on his own account, had not neglected Jessie. Blanche was surprised at her knowledge and quick intelligence.

Cecil was obliged to be out that day, but

when he came in he did his best to enter-
tain the little girl, jumping her up almost
as high as their low ceiling, and marching
about with the child on his shoulder, re-
collecting that that was the manner Ben
had accommodated her on his first visit to
their home; all which Jessie fully enjoyed,
with the *abandon* of mirth and laughter
that little children are blessed with.

Mrs. Brewster had engaged to take her
safely home, but before she went Blanche
made her a present, that she and Sally
Brewster had manufactured between them,
of a pretty little frock and jacket. Among
all the gifts she had made, none had afforded her so much pleasure, perhaps because it had cost her some trouble. In
the tiny pocket was stuffed half-a-pound
of tobacco for Ben, with her brother's
kind regards.

After this Sunday, several days of bad
weather kept Blanche to the house, and
she was unable to see her new little pet;

but at last the cold wind and rain passed off, and it became clear, though frosty. Cecil was very busy as the time of his short absence approached, and stayed out till late; but Blanche was determined, after one of his most fatiguing days, that he should have a comfortable evening and carry away with him a cheerful remembrance of his cottage home.

That night Blanche and Cecil were sitting over their bright wood fire; the little neat cottage room looked pleasant in the warm, red light. Blanche had coaxed a fine tabby kitten to take up its residence with them, and it now joined their party and sat purring on the rug, the image of content, until, from a sudden impulse of affection, which cats do possess contrary to the opinion of some people, she lightly leapt on Cecil's knee.

"It is odd that Penelope *will* like you best," said Blanche, who had given this name to her kitten on account of the virtuous propriety of its demeanour and its excellent domestic character; "I know these creatures have a kind of wizard-like intuitive knowledge of the human heart; now Penclope knows as well as possible how kind and gentle you are."

"Poor Pen!" said Cecil, stroking her down softly. "It is very comfortable here, Blanche, is it not?"

"But what do you think of my having prepared a little dissipation for to-night? We are to indulge in an excess."

And running into the small kitchen, she came out smiling with a steaming hot jug in her hand.

"Now, then, what do you think? Hot negus! Will it not be good, and send us to bed happy?"

And with a joyous laugh she put it on a round table between them, while Mrs. Brewster, who had been in the house busy looking up and packing Cecil's things, followed with a tray, some glasses, and toast.

"Mrs. Brewster," said Blanche, "you must wish my brother a happy journey, and try our brew."

So saying, she poured out a good tumblerful for the worthy woman, who smiled and curtseyed, only just putting her lips to it for manners' sake, and wishing Mr. "Charles" a lucky journey, retired with her spoils.

The brother and sister sat up late, chatting and warming themselves, until Blanche insisted that as Cecil had to get up very early the next morning he should go to bed, and she would soon follow his example.

About a quarter of an hour afterwards Mrs. Brewster came in to the parlour.

"I am so sorry, Miss, my husband has just been up here, and he says Ben Darley's little girl, little Jessie, has had the fever very bad two or three days, and is not like to live."

Blanche turned sharp round.

" Little Jessie ?"

" Yes, poor little dear ! And what'll happen to poor Ben, I don't know; he does so dote on the little thing. Brewster called there as he came home. He was out late to-night after some of Squire Bingham's horses, and as he went by he see a light in Ben's window. So he went in and see the little thing. She asked after you, Miss.

" What did she say ?" inquired Blanche.

" Oh, well she did say she wanted very bad to see pretty lady—she always calls you ' pitty lady !' She has a fancy she shan't see you again, without she sees you to-night, Miss."

" She wishes to see me to-night, then ?"

" Well, poor little thing, you know, Miss, they as is not long for this world do have strange fancies by times."

" Would you mind going with me, Mrs. Brewster ?"

" I ?—Lord bless you, no, Miss. I often go out nursing. But it's late for you—it's nigh upon twelve."

" Never mind ; we will go," said Blanche.

And quietly she stole up to her room, not to disturb Cecil, and put her things on.

" Is it a fine night ?" she inquired, the least in the world frightened at her strange expedition.

" Beautiful, Miss," said Mrs. Brewster.

" Do you think she would like a little of this ?" she said, pointing to the negus.

" It's beautiful," said Mrs. Brewster. " It might revive her a bit, if she could take a spoonful or two."

And she put a little in a small bottle.

" I suppose Ben would not think it an intrusion ?" inquired Blanche.

" Ben, Ma'am ? Lord bless you ! My old man he said, ' Would you like her to come ?'—meaning you, Ma'am. And he, Ben, said, 'Ay should I, if she do '—meaning Jessie; ' but it ain't to be expected.' "

The moment they stepped outside a keen air blew in her face. She looked around. All on earth was dark, but above the sky was bright, the stars shone vividly.

"Too bright to last," Mrs. Brewster said.

"I wish I had known before that little Jessie was ill," Blanche said.

"Well, Miss, I see the child the other day. She looked tired-like, and was lying on Ben's lap, but I didn't think much of it. Ben said, 'I'm afraid she's ill, Mrs. Brewster,' and I says, 'You are too much set on the child. She'll be well enough soon; but you make a idol of the child, and you hadn't ought. ' I may love my own child,' says Ben, ' and I will too.' And as he began to look black at me I went away, not thinking much of the child's being poorly. Children is so often a little ailing, as I knows well, and you'll know, too, to your cost some day, Miss. Lord! when my Betsy had the measles, her face looked like a clover field in full bloom. And there was our Sally, as lives with you, Ma'am, she had the whooping-cough, and for two months the house was shook as with an earthquake every time as she coughed, poor dear!"

This style of conversation Blanche did not object to, for it made the way appear less lonely; but she did not at all like it when Mrs. Brewster — indulging in the taste for horrors that common people have to a great extent, especially sick-nurses, who like topers require something a little strong to excite them—began talking of corpse-lights, and coffins, and shrouds, and all the dismal concomitants of poor mortality. Besides, as she so talked the sky darkened, a moaning wind sprang up, and the stars seemed extinguished.

"Ay, we shall have a downfall," said Mrs. Brewster, looking round, as they reached the lonely cottage.

"A downfall?" said Blanche, nervously. "Why—how?"

"Oh, of snow, Miss. It's too late in the season for snow, by rights. March snow brings a cold May; and you mark my words, Miss, there'll be death nigh when that snow falls."

Blanche gently opened the cottage door, and entering went straight to Jessie's room.

In it there was a lamp alight, and Ben was sitting by the bedside, with his elbow on his knee and his head resting on his hand, gazing earnestly at the little girl, who was lying still and pale, with her large dark eyes turned on his.

Little as Blanche knew of such symptoms, she saw instantly a change that

spoke too plainly to be mistaken; the seal
of death was on the little faded face. Ben
only slightly raised his head as she entered,
but Jessie gave a little weak cry of joy,
and spread out her arms towards Blanche,
who came forward to the side of the bed
opposite to where Ben was seated, and
stooped down to the child, who put out her
lips for a kiss, and her arms round the
neck of Blanche, who bent down and
kissed her tenderly.

" Dear lady, Jessie love dear lady," she
said faintly.

Blanche caressed her, then glanced at
Ben.

" Has she had a doctor ?"

"Yes, and that's the stuff," he answered,
turning to a small table with a bottle of
medicine and a cup ; " and she should have
a nurse too, but she don't like no nurse,
except me."

Jessie turned her eyes to him, and put

out her little limp hand to her father with a contented smile.

"Jessie love papa," she said, as if she almost feared lest he should be jealous of her love for Blanche.

Blanche gave her a little of the negus; she liked it, but could only swallow a tea-spoonful or two.

"Give papa some," she said. To satisfy her, Ben tasted it.

"Jessie go to the angels," she said to Blanche, with a solemn but happy look in her eyes. "Jessie saw beautiful angels," and she raised her eyes upwards in so rapt a gaze, and with so heavenly a smile, that Blanche could scarcely avoid believing that she really saw what she spoke of.

"No, not yet, Jessie; don't go yet!" said her father.

"Papa come too—papa come to Jessie— will papa come to Jessie?" she said, in a tone of such tender entreaty that the man's burning eyes filled with tears; she turned towards him and stroked slowly and lovingly his dark face and whiskers.

"You know who lives up there—who is good—who loves papa and Jessie—you know."

"Are you happy, Jessie?" he asked.

"Oh! so happy, but . . . . . not like other days, but more happy; when will it be to-morrow?"

"It is two o'clock," said Blanche, looking at her watch.

"It is a long way to to-morrow," said the child, and she seemed in deep thought. "Papa must be happy, will he? Jessie will be far off, but she will never forget papa."

Ben covered his face with both his hands and wept.

"No," said the child, distressed, "not cry, papa," and again she did her best, stroking and petting him.

"Papa," she said, trying to pull his hands away, and with a bright smile— "Papa!"

He looked at her—to him it seemed that she was already one of those angels she thought she had seen.

"Oh, papa!" and with a sudden spring, and a strength that startled Blanche, she threw herself into his arms, with her little face on his shoulder. He sat motionless, holding to his beating heart her silent pulseless heart.

Blanche gently went round and looked down on her. All was still, the happy little spirit had flown; she softly endeavoured to take the child from the father's arms.

"Not yet," he said, in a tone of agony, "oh! not yet."

Blanche sat down silent on the bedside, her tears streaming fast.

"Let me take her," at last she said, gently.

He looked at her a moment bewildered,

and then resigned the little form, which Blanche laid tenderly on the bed.

Poor Ben looked once on the cold, little white face, then throwing himself on his knees by the bed, smothered his head in the counterpane. Blanche remained some time, then rose and touched him.

"Ben," she said.

He started, he had forgotten that she was there, he had forgotten everything except his child.

"I will come to you to-morrow, shall I?"

"If you please, Madam," he answered in a husky tone.

"Remember," said Blanche, "she is happy."

"Ah!" he said, "I never deserved her."

"There is not one of us who ever does deserve the blessings we enjoy, but, Ben, I cannot bear to see you in such grief."

"You are very good, Madam," he said,

" but mine is one that'll last my life. I
shall never forget her."

" No; but think of her as she is—an
angel."

So saying she left him, and followed by
Mrs. Brewster went out of the cottage, still
weeping.

It was indeed as Mrs. Brewster had pro-
phesied; the snow was on the ground, a
white sheet was spread over the fields, and
shone ghastly in the livid cold light of a
wintry dawn; as they passed along the
wood side each tree bore its frozen burden,
each little twig had its small weight of
snow to bear—all was shrouded and
deathly, Blanche thought, beneath the dull
grey sky.

She entered the Forest Lodge and went
up to her room so quietly that Cecil never
even awoke, and in ten minutes, quite worn
out with fatigue, was asleep.

Mrs. Brewster took care to keep the house
quiet; and when Blanche arose she was

surprised to find Cecil already gone out. Mrs. Brewster good-naturedly persuaded her to have her breakfast up-stairs. Cecil returned home as soon as he could.

" Dear Blanche," he said, " I was so sorry to hear about poor little Jessie ; and what a night you had ! Why did you not call me ? I had much rather have gone there with you ; I could have stayed in the other room."

" Most certainly not," she replied ; " you have plenty to do in the day, without walking about all night out of your proper business."

" Besides I know," said Cecil, " you do not like those melancholy scenes."

" I must own," Blanche answered, " that though I have pretty good courage where there's something to be done or overcome, I am not fond of sitting by and seeing dreadful things. Good gracious ! I remember now and then, when I used to go and see some of the old women about

Crown-Harden who were very ill, I used to be so afraid lest they should die before I could get out of the way; but this was quite different," and Blanche's expression changed to a gentle seriousness that it did not often wear. "I am glad I was there, Cecil; dear little Jessie was so happy; it gave a new light to what had appeared to me before all darkness. Only poor Ben!"

The snow was now melting fast in a warm thaw, and a hundred trickling steamlets ran down the hill-side; in the evening a mild yellow light was diffused through the air, and Blanche stepped outside.

"I will go up and see Ben," she said.

Cecil made no objection, and the two walked there together, more grave than usual. Mrs. Brewster, who was there, came out and took her at once to the room where little Jessie lay—a little waxen image only, but sweet and placid. If she had been pretty before, she was beautiful now.

Ben sat by her side, looking at her as he had on the last night—no longer agitated, but in deep, silent sorrow.

Blanche advanced gently and touched the ice-cold brow with her lips. She took up a lock of Jessie's silken hair.

" May I ?" she asked.

Ben only bent his head, and she cut off a piece, and folding it up, put it inside her dress. Ben looked at her with a melancholy smile; he liked her for doing it.

She remained there a few minutes, and then saying kindly, " Good-bye, Ben," she went out again to the kitchen, where Mrs. Brewster was sitting.

" Do they want money ?" she whispered.

" No, no, they don't, Miss."

" Well, in case they do," and Blanche put a half-sovereign into her hand. Soon after Cecil came in, and they returned homewards.

" Shall you go to the funeral, Blanche ?" he asked.

" I think so," she replied.

" Then I will stay till it is over; I could not leave you alone."

" No, Cecil, do not think of it; Sir Philip Holland is an odd man, if you lose your holiday, he may not give you another."

" I will not leave you," he repeated. " Mrs. Brewster tells me he was kind to Ben; as soon as he heard of Jessie's illness he sent Mrs. Arnicott, the housekeeper, down with all kinds of good things, though the little darling could scarcely touch them."

Cecil was not obliged to postpone his visit to Crown-Harden, for the funeral took place the day before he left; so Mrs. Brewster arranged it, and Ben passively submitted to have all as she thought best.

" It isn't a day or so more that'll make the difference," he said quietly.

Blanche did attend the funeral of her little favourite; she felt that choking sensation all know too well, when the sound of the earth falling on the little coffin reached her ear. She dared not look at Ben, who stood there pale and motionless.

Cecil came to meet her at the church-yard gate. They waited a few minutes till the father came out, but he did not see them at first—he saw nothing but that little grave before his eyes. When Cecil spoke he touched his hat. Without saying a word Cecil wrung his hand, and Ben turned his head away; but though he could not speak, his heart was full of gratitude to both sister and brother.

"Ben," said Cecil, "I have to leave my sister, she is not used to be alone, but you will come to see her once or twice, I know, and see that she is safe."

"That I will," said Ben, "she's next to my own, because " . . . .

"I understand you," said Cecil, and they parted with feelings widely opposed to those they had experienced on their first meeting.

Little Jessie on her death-bed had sown seeds that were received into a sincere and truthful heart, and they were not thrown away. From that night Ben was, we do not say an altered man, Nature is not wholly changed, but may be turned into an entirely new direction. Hitherto Ben's had been a wrong one, he knew it and gloried in it, but now, though he could not believe it himself, his path had turned towards a different goal.

"She bid me come to her," he said to Blanche, who with the skill and delicacy of a woman had led him to speak of his child the first time he came to see her, "but it can't be, it is not likely for a poor bad fellow like me to get up there."

"Why not?" said Blanche.

"I'm only fit to go groping about in the dark, and go where it's darker yet," he answered.

Then Blanche spoke of those things

that we can realize only when the heart is full, but which cannot be touched on here, with earnest but perfect simplicity.

CHAPTER XVII.

ON the afternoon before Cecil started for his visit to Crown-Harden, the brother and sister took a long ramble in the woods together.

It was a lovely Spring day. Some of the early leaves had unfolded, the dew-drops glittered on the blades of grass in the narrow woodland alley, clusters of violets sent up a sudden puff of incense here and there as they passed; primroses spangled the shady places, the westering sun dappled with amber all the places he touched, while a soft, dim shadow fell in mysterious obscurity on the farther bowery recesses into which their eyes could not penetrate.

In the distance a wood-pigeon softly cooed its mate to repose, and the tap of the wood-pecker was not yet silenced.

"The fairy bands are mustering," said Blanche, "and there is the tiny roll of their drum. We will not go home till the moon has risen. There is a lovely large round moon; I saw it last night."

In due time a redness tinged the darkening sky. All was hushed and silent, and the two stood still with a sensation of awe. A broad, blood-red globe shone amid the trees, and very slowly, but majestically, the moon rose into the air, sending a faint radiance athwart the stems and trunks of the forest. Much sooner than it seemed possible she was high in the velvet blue sky, while here and there a diamond-lustred star looked down upon them through the leaves.

Blanche drew a deep breath.

"Oh, Cecil," she said, "at times like this one feels how very inferior one is to

the many glorious things God has made.
I have sometimes wished to be less un-
worthy."

"My own darling Blanche!" Cecil said,
affectionately, pressing her arm to his side,
"if we feel like this, and do not stop there,
what we have suffered will be really for
our good. One is often told that all is for
the best, but only rarely one feels it."

"Dear Cecil," said Blanche, "take care
of yourself when you are away. You are
the only dear thing left me. Without you,
oh, think how desolate I should be!"

"My child," he said, looking down on
her and smiling, her face, and his, too,
looking lily-white in the moonlight, "just
consider, I am only going for three days,
or perhaps four, and no farther than
Crown-Harden. I might be on the eve
of a journey to the Arctic Sea."

"Yes, yes, I know it is silly. Still, do
remember—remember above all your promise about Stephen Granville."

"I do," he said, "and will keep it, however inconvenient it may prove. Now are you satisfied?"

"We will go home," she said. "What a lovely walk we have had! My head is almost dizzy with so much beauty."

Cecil's visit and journey will take so much time to relate, that it will be well to see how the time passed with Blanche—for Cecil did not come back either in three days, or four.

Unknown to either brother or sister, much speculation was afloat in the neighbourhood regarding them, and even reached the ears of Sir Philip Holland. The unusual beauty of Blanche, by attracting much attention, was no advantage to her now, and there were various circumstances that appeared suspicious about her to inquisitive eyes.

Mrs. Brewster, who did her washing, had been out one week and had engaged a woman for the work, who was not only a frequent assistant and ally to the two Miss Tripleys, whose caps peeping forth from the house near the inn had annoyed Blanche, but she was often employed by the housekeeper at Holland Abbey, who was an intimate friend of the gossiping Miss Tripley's.

When drinking tea at their house, waited on by the officious charwoman, she was entertained with exaggerated accounts of Blanche's fine lady habits; how when poor dear Mrs. Andrews, the late gamekeeper's wife, used to curtsey respectfully, and make room for the Miss Tripleys to go out of church before them, Blanche marched out first, as if they were nobody, and she the queen of the place; but worse was to come—she then heard from the lips of the charwoman how the articles of dress she had got up for Blanche were as grand, as fine, as beautiful, as my Lady's own, all trimmed with lace and embroidery. Her body-linen, as it was elegantly called, must have cost a fortune, her night-dresses a guinea a piece if they cost a penny. Was it likely that a well-conducted young woman would have such clothes?

"I can tell you more, too," said the woman; "she is no more his sister than I am. Most of her things are marked with initials, but there were two or three marked in full, and the name was not Crawford, that I'll take my Bible oath, though I can't tell what it was—I can't just remember."

"Dear me, can't you? what a pity!". was the rejoinder.

"I could tell you a secret, too; but I don't know that I ought, for it concerns them as belongs to the great folks here."

"Ought!" cried all, in chorus, "of course you ought! it's your bounden duty."

"Well, Ma'am, since you say so. In the pocket of a muslin dress she sent one day when the weather got so hot, was the cover of a letter, only the cover, you know, and who do you think it was directed to?—To the Hon. Henry Villeroy, and the rest of the direction in full."

"What an abandoned creature! and to dare to come here! I see how it all is, it's too clear—it's dreadful!"

Mrs. Arnicott, the housekeeper, on her return to Holland Abbey, communicated to her master, who she well knew liked to be informed of all that passed, the discoveries she had made, not as suspicions but certainties; and Sir Philip's misanthropic, suspicious disposition caused him to embrace, without hesitation, the same evil constructions, especially as he thought that Cecil's handsome face and appearance were well calculated to catch the fancy of an unprincipled girl.

Blanche, meanwhile, during two of the weary twenty-four hours after Cecil's departure, did not leave the house or see anyone but good old Barty and his wife and daughter.

On the third day, having had no news of her brother, she went out in the garden to gather a few early flowers and was startled by seeing at the gate a man on a stout grey cob; she immediately remembered the description of Sir Philip Holland, and knew that it was he.

Without the slightest ceremony, or waiting to be invited, he deliberately got off his horse, hung the bridle on the gate, and walked up the gravel path to her; she slightly bowed, he made a movement, indicating that he would follow her into the house, to which, being unable to prevent it, she assented.

He shut the parlour door after him, sat down, and taking his eye-glass, examined her at his leisure. She also sat down at some little distance, and as a matter of prudence near the door, for she began to fancy he must be mad.

"Hum" — he began, "are you the young man's wife?"

" No," she answered, " his sister."

" Sister ? — Oh ! sister," he repeated, with a sneering smile. " I wish to inform you, young woman, that I am very particular as to the conduct of my dependents— very particular indeed."

" Quite right !" said Blanche, her temper rising to very near boiling point, " it is to be hoped you are equally particular about your own."

He stared at her in amazement. " You have some trifling amount of—of assurance," he observed. Seeing that Blanche made no answer, he continued, " I understood that Charles Crawford was to return to-day."

The sound was unfamiliar to the ears of Blanche, but she instantly remembered that was the name her brother had adopted.

" Being his *sister*, I presume you are what ?—Bella Crawford ? Am I to under-

stand that your name is Bertha?—Bella?
—Bessie Crawford?"

"I should think your name was Paul
Pry," muttered Blanche in a rage. His
ears were quicker than his eyes.

"Paul Pry?—good indeed! a lady of
so sportive a spirit may well sport an
alias. I know that your name is not
Crawford."

Blanche coloured deeply, she was very
angry, but unfortunately she was embarrassed also, so that her expression might
well have been mistaken for guilt by a
person less suspicious than Sir Philip
Holland.

"I most sincerely hope that your situation here is a perfectly respectable one,"
said he gravely, "a perfectly, unquestion-
ably respectable one; I do hope you are
this young man's sister, not his" . . . .

"Leave the room, Sir," said Blanche
imperiously, "leave the house, Sir, and
never dare to show your particularly dis-

pleasing face here again, as long as we remain."

" I had fancied, young lady, that your —your brother or cousin, we will say *brother*, was my gamekeeper, my servant; pray may I venture to ask *what* your brother is?"

"What you never were—a gentleman !" exclaimed Blanche, indignantly, in the heat of her wrath; but the instant the unguarded word had escaped her, she could have bit the tip of her tongue off. " A gentleman in thought and feeling," she added, endeavouring to correct her mistake.

" Oh, indeed ! a gentleman you say ! Oh ! I see, a gentleman."

Blanche looked down, colouring with vexation. He took his eye-glass again, and once more coolly examined her.

" Then of course you are a lady," he said at last. " I had heard some reports greatly to your disadvantage, young *lady*," putting a strong emphasis on the word,

" I now believe them to be false, and so believing, nothing remains to me but most humbly to beg your pardon. Pray may I hope that you deign to grant it ?"

And getting up from his chair, he made her a most magnificent bow.

" You are a very odd man," she said. " Well, I do grant it ?"

" Spoken right royally," said the gentleman. " Madam, I intrude no longer; you have very unequivocally shown me the door, and I go out by it."

" If you choose to behave properly, I revoke my order," she said; but at the same time opening the door for him, while he bowed himself out, repeating as he went,

" A real beauty, face, figure, and all —a real beauty !"

It was not until he had closed the door behind him, that he remembered that he had omitted to reproach her for the unflattering comments on himself that he had overheard some time ago in the wood, so as he passed the window he tapped at the lattice.

" I must see you on business to-morrow morning, young girl.   Do you hear ?"

Blanche nodded rather saucily, and Sir Philip took his departure.

Early the following morning according to his promise he marched up the gravel walk, and unceremoniously tapped at the casement.   Blanche did not admire such very easy manners, and therefore merely looked up at the window without taking farther notice.

Sir Philip presently went and tapped at the door, when Mrs. Brewster opened it, and solemnly ushered him in.

" You would not come to me at the window ?" he said.

" In England people do not pay visits through the window," she answered.

" Ah ! true—well I will come to business,

young lady. I come to ask you what business you had in the wood the other day to call me an ugly monster of a man, and the old Ogre of the Abbey?"

"I had just as much right to call you so," said Blanche, not in the least discomposed, "as you had to listen to me. Listeners never hear any good of themselves, you know."

"But," returned Sir Philip, "I was an involuntary listener."

"Why did not you cough, or sneeze, or blow your nose," said Blanche, "as a gentleman you ought."

"Then I will do so now," said he, blowing his nose very sonorously, perhaps to hide a trifling embarrassment.

"Besides," rejoined Blanche, with her arch smile, "you know I had never seen you then."

"Meaning that you would be more charitable now, young lady?"

Blanche glanced at him slyly, he had

left off the great red comforter round his neck and assumed a more dandy style of bluffness.

"Pray do not call me young lady," Blanche remarked, "I wear this brown stuff gown on purpose not."

"On you I thought it was brown velvet —would you like a brown velvet?"

"No, not at all—it would be in curious taste in this little cottage; this dress cost just seven and ninepence."

"An interesting fact!" replied Sir Philip, satirically. "So handsome a girl, if I am not to say young lady," continued he, "must wish for correspondingly hand-some men to admire her—I fear you will find none about here."

"Well ... I ... I am not so sure of that," said Blanche, a little timidly.

"Indeed! where do they live, pray?"

"I should think," answered Blanche demurely, "about a mile and a half from the Lodge here."

This was exactly the distance from Holland Abbey.

" A mile and a half—hum—is this handsome man of the same rank as yourself!"

" Oh, no! Oh, dear no!" replied Blanche.

" Is he young?"

" No, not exactly young; at least not very."

" And really handsome?" inquired Sir Philip with animation.

" If not strictly handsome, a very fine man—a *very* striking appearance."

" You make me curious," said Sir Philip; " may one know his name?"

" I hardly know whether—whether I—" hesitated Blanche, as if in slight confusion; " but perhaps if you really wish me . . ."

" I really do, and very much indeed."

" Since you say so," said Blanche mischievously, " I mean Ben Darley."

Sir Philip jumped up in a rage and stamped furiously.

" You little Jezebel!" then bursting out

laughing, he added, " Why did you not say *me* ?"

" Oh !" said Blanche, who had risen suddenly, a little startled at the ebullition, which was rather stronger than she had anticipated, and curtseying with pretty little affectation :

" I would not have taken such a liberty."

" Why, I used to be a very handsome man !"

" An interesting fact," laughed Blanche, mimicking Sir Philip's manner of saying the words.

" You are a bewitching little—what am I to call you ? What *is* your name—for I know it is not Crawford."

" Ah !" said Blanche, " I see that we cannot preserve our secret, though it is indeed a very innocent one."

" Why do you look at me with those blue eyes brimming with tears ? What do you want ?"

" To ask you as a gentleman not to

penetrate our poor little secret," Blanche
replied.

"Well, to please you I won't. What
else?"

"If you are kind to my brother, you
will be handsome, and graceful, and everything else in my eyes."

"You are a self-interested little monkey,
I am afraid; one word for me and two for
yourself—the way of the world."

"I suppose *you* never think of yourself,
Sir Philip Holland?" asked Blanche, with
a little arch look.

"Yes, I do; and of very little else; I
am an old despot—a lawless tyrant—
accustomed, ogre as I am, to live here,
monarch of all I survey, and see everybody
ready to obey and defer to me. I am
rough, selfish, like to frighten people, care
for nobody; would not lose my cigar, or
my good dinner, or my good wine, to save
the life of my best friend; so now perhaps
you know me, don't you?"

"I should find out a good deal more than that," said Blanche.

"Indeed! of what kind—good or bad? Come, be an honest girl—tell me."

"No, I won't," said Blanche; "if I find you out, you must find me out; as far as my opinion of you goes, I give you leave— no further."

"I believe you rather like me?" inquired Sir Philip.

"That is not the way to find out," laughed Blanche, shaking her head ominously, for she was born to be a coquette.

"It certainly would be a very important discovery," said Sir Philip sarcastically. "Well, good-bye; I wish you better; don't try to coquette with me."

"Indeed, Sir Philip," said Blanche, putting on an air of great candour, "I only wanted to amuse you a little; your life must be so very, very dull."

"*Petite impertinente!*" he exclaimed, and sweeping the floor with his hat, which he snatched up, making her a mock-heroic bow, he marched off.

" I do rather like him," said Blanche to herself; " there's something of the old lion about him."

CHAPTER XIX.

IN the evening after Sir Philip Holland's visit, Blanche felt unwell and depressed. She was unused to be left in solitude; her head ached, and she gently opened the house-door, and paced along the grass border on the side of the gravel walk.

The moon had lately risen, but the whole length of the straight walk and the lower portion of the garden were in deep shadow, while a white mist dimmed the parts that lay in moonlight. She suddenly stopped short, fancying she heard a rustling. Yes, there was a stealthy footstep. Her heart beat violently. She stood near a large old apple-tree, and at her side grew a thick laurustinus. She wore a dark dress, not likely to be seen, and stooped down to conceal herself. Something moved in the bushes at the farther end of the small garden. She hardly knew how to bear the suspense — she almost longed to spring like a tigress on the spy, whosoever he might be.

Stop!—there she perceived the figure of a man creeping step by step nearer to her. Skirting along the shaded side of the walk, he passed close by her, and advanced towards the windows of her house. Cautiously glancing round, he peeped in, then crept cat-like round to the back.

Instantly seizing the opportunity, Blanche, swift and silent as a shadow, flew to the door, opened it noiselessly, and entering went straight to the kitchen, where the Brewster family was preparing for bed after a hearty supper of broiled bacon.

" There is some one watching round the house !" exclaimed Blanche. " There at the back."

Old Brewster, roaring out threats, seized the poker, and burst forth, while the two women stared in terror.

Soon he came in again.

"Bless you, Miss! there's nothing, nor nobody."

" There was," said Blanche, in that tone that carries conviction.

" Well, Miss, if you're frighted in the night, you call me, that's all," said honest Barty.

Blanche had more reason to be " frighted " than he could dream of, for she had caught a momentary glimpse of the face in the dim moonlight, and she felt sure it was the ill-omened face of Orlando Henshawe.

She passed a wretched night; she never even thought of sleep; she scarcely rested her head on the pillow a moment. With nerves in an agonised state of tension, unaccustomed to sleeplessness and anxiety, the excitement and fever of the brain were so strange to her that every kind of terrible fancy possessed her by turn.

In the day-time she had not thought much of the delay in Cecil's return, and of his not writing. He used to have the bad habit of being unpunctual in his engagements; but now, as she reflected, he had more thought—he was more considerate. She could scarcely believe he would leave her in this suspense without some cause. And what was the meaning of Orlando Henshawe's secret visit? Why was he prowling around the house in so deceitful a style? With strained ears, and eyes staring into the unresponding obscurity, hours passed. A strange chilling horror came over her, so unknown to all her former experience, that she believed it must be a fatal presentiment.

" Oh, Cecil," she said, though she knew not she was speaking aloud, " alive or dead, come to me. If you live no longer, I do not fear, let your spirit visit me !"

Then she thought she heard at intervals sounds below, outside, she scarce knew where.

The grey dawn stole in quietly as a ghost, glimmering pale, when objects began to take shape and form, though unlike that which they assumed in daylight; a chirp or two was heard from a bird outside, followed by the uncertain whispered sounds and rustlings that precede morning; and how thankful she was when the distant snoring of Barty Brewster ceased and she heard movement in the house. How gladly she at once got up and dressed, finding that broad daylight, movement, and the common occupations of life chased away the horrors of the dark hours, though they still left her pale, anxious and languid. She had half intended to take a walk to the village church, and visit Jessie's little grave; but she altered her determination, she felt

that her spirits required rather what
might raise them than what might increase their depression.

CHAPTER XX.

AN overpowering sentiment of mingled pain and delight filled the mind of Cecil as the old familiar home of his boyhood came into view; he felt as if he had been banished for years, instead of months, and regret and affection moved him by turns.

As soon as he entered the house, he was shown up at once into the library, where Rosamond was lying on the sofa. She sprang up to meet him with an expression of unfeigned joy. Her cheeks glowed, her large soul-speaking eyes filled with soft lustre.

"Dear Cecil! how good, how kind of you to come. Oh! it makes me so happy. I sometimes have thought—"

She stopped short, turned pale, and seemed unable to support herself. Cecil gently assisted her to the sofa.

"I told you I had been unwell, but I am better," she said, as he sat looking at her in some consternation; for she was much changed, far more lovely, but more fragile in appearance.

"I hope you are better," he said anxiously.

"A great deal," she answered. "I know you promised to come, but I could hardly persuade myself that you really would. Oh, Cecil, it is very kind of you."

Cecil found it difficult to sit with composure and hear himself so praised and thanked, and Rosamond could little guess what a flood of passionate words rose from his heart to his lips, and died there because he must not utter them.

She felt, however, that there was some slight constraint on his part.

"Have you quite—quite forgiven me, Cecil?" she said, leaning her graceful head towards him.

"Have I forgiven?" he exclaimed, and bending down, he hid his face on the arm of her sofa. Only for a minute, when with an effort he determined to shake off the agitating emotion of a first meeting with feelings so widely altered.

"I hope you can make some stay?" she asked, with a touch of her old timidity.

"Only a day or two," Cecil answered.

"Tell me," she inquired, "how is Blanche?"

"Very well, thank you, Rosamond, and merry, she says."

"Thank heaven for that!" she exclaimed, earnestly. "Will you ring? you will not mind having your dinner brought up here, will you?"

"Not at all," was the answer.

Dinner soon appeared. Cecil was surprised to find how changed Rosamond was; no longer silent and moody, she talked with animation, she was as lively as Blanche herself; but there was a something that Blanche had not—a very indescribable, fugitive, evanescent something, like the delicate aroma of some exquisite perfume that had been present and was not quite dispersed. It was the almost imperceptible charm of a most poetic, ardent, and tender nature which had hitherto been bound down . in hard restraint. Cecil felt it, though he hardly understood it.

" You do not ask after dear old Don Ricardo," said Rosamond.

" I have been expecting to see him make his appearance every moment," Cecil replied.

" It is such a pity, he left us about a week ago. He has long been wishing to look after some concerns of his, but did not like to leave me till I got stronger. I

wish he had delayed one more week. The
more you know him, the more you love
him. Ah, Cecil! I wish he were rich! he
is very fond of you and Blanche. That is
one reason why I am so fond of him."

" And your brother ?" inquired Cecil.

Rosamond's brightness faded away.

" Ah !" she said, sighing, " he is not
what I wish; but I hope he will be away
still for some time. He is very bad."

" I am bound," said Cecil, " to go at
once if he returns here ; Blanche made me
promise faithfully that I would, so you
must not be offended, Rosamond. I suppose that she was afraid I should be violent
if there were any disagreement, but I assure you I am improved; I have learnt a
few lessons since you saw me last."

Rosamond could not speak, but the tears
fell fast; her feeling heart could ill endure
the thought of the proud, gay Cecil learning
such hard lessons; yet she knew he had
needed them. But she thrust aside, at

least for the present, all that could sadden her. She wished above all that he should enjoy the few days he spent in his old home.

After dinner Cecil went down and looked round, spoke to Mrs. Benson and a few old servants, took a few turns round the garden with Rosamond, who rejoined him there; then returned to the library and spent the evening with her.

The next morning, in the course of conversation, former times were reverted to, and their uncle was mentioned.

"Cecil," she said, "I wanted you to see his last letter to me; it says some cruel things, which I can hardly bear to show you, yet, from the way he acted, you must guess what he felt, and though they must distress you, it"——

"It will be only what I expect," said Cecil, finishing the sentence for her.

"I hope," said Rosamond, "it will justify me in your eyes, or, at least, clear me of the guilt of wilfully injuring you; that is what I most desire in the world."

She was lying on the sofa, for she was always more weak and languid in the morning.

" The letters are in the cabinet, in the study," she said, " might I ask you to bring them ?"

Cecil rose immediately, and Rosamond took the silver key that hung from her waist by a stout silver chain, and was dropped into her dress pocket, unfastened it by a padlock that was opened by a tiny key attached to her watch-chain, and gave the key of the cabinet to Cecil.

" The third drawer on the left-hand side, there are two or three letters tied with a green ribbon."

Cecil, entering the study, followed her directions; it took some minutes to open the cabinet, find the drawer, and lock all up as before.

When he re-entered the library he was

not much pleased to see Orlando Henshawe standing there.

He gave a slight nod to Henshawe, and returned the silver key to Rosamond, still holding the packet of letters in his hand, while Orlando Henshawe stood scrutinizing him keenly.

"Did you understand that my brother is not yet returned, Mr. Henshawe?" said Rosamond haughtily. "I will not detain you."

"Oh, certainly," he answered with a confident air, "certainly; but Stephen will be here before long. I have heard from him."

"Good morning," said Rosamond, bending her head with great stateliness.

"Oh, indeed! Good morning; good morning, Miss Granville," and with a spiteful leer at Cecil, the gentleman left the room.

"Odious man!" said Rosamond; "he encourages Stephen in all that is bad."

"Is your brother likely to return to-day ?" asked Cecil.

"Oh, no, I dare say not," she answered; "he had no doubt found out that you were here, and merely made the excuse to come and spy about. At all events, Mrs. Benson never shows Stephen in to me; I go down to him in the dining-room when I wish to see him. He understands that he is not to disturb me up here. Here is the letter, Cecil;" and as he took it she again fastened the key on to the silver chain. Cecil smiled at such extreme precaution.

"Mr. Henshawe desired me never to let this key go out of my own hands, especially until he has drawn up the copies of the will and done what is necessary. I wish he would, but he is so dilatory and has been ill again, poor man; he would feel hurt if we employed anyone else. He told me if anything happened to the will, no one would be benefited, but it would entail much trouble and distress."

Rosamond did not think it necessary to repeat the lawyer's representations that, if it were missing, many witnesses could attest to its existence and contents, law proceedings must be taken, and suspicion would fall on every member of the family. She knew that these hints pointed at Stephen Granville, who had expressed great discontent at the disposal of the property, in so far as his sister was preferred to himself.

"Will you read the letter?" she said, . giving it to her cousin.

It ran as follows :

"I am not strong enough, my child, to discuss verbally the point at issue between us. Any discussion agitates and fatigues me. I appreciate your generous and passionate advocacy of your cousins' claims and merits, and comprehend your repugnance to usurp their places in my favour.

You are also, I doubt not, equally sincere in declaring that riches would never add to your happiness, but might cause your misery. You think so now, my little Rosamond, but I have lived in the world longer than you—and you will not always be eighteen. If it were really for your happiness, and as you so earnestly desire to shrink from the position I would place you in, I might leave my money to a charity; but to that nephew and niece of mine whose name blisters my lips, and my fingers refuse to write—never; their ingratitude has broken my heart. I overheard those cruel words, when she wished me dead that I might weary her no more. I came down with no intention to overhear, but goaded by an impatient uncertainty regarding my will. I was then stronger, better; I might have lived, but those words were my death-blow; therefore, Rosamond, say no more, or you will kill me too; and, be my decision what it

may, you, poor child, will never alter it
in the slightest degree."

Cecil turned pale as he read these
accusations against himself and his sister.

"Then it was my uncle you saw standing at the study-door?" he asked.

"It was, alas!" said Rosamond. "Oh,
Cecil! I could not bear to show you this
heart-rending letter before—even though
I thought it might replace me in your
esteem. But I have thought I should die,
and I could not go away, and leave so
black a stain upon my memory. Our
uncle wrote this letter in a moment of
fierce anger against you. I am sure he
felt more justly afterwards. He knew
those were only thoughtless, unmeaning
words. In spite of his prohibition I did
once say so, and he made a gesture of
assent, and at the last he forgave you—
he longed for you—he loved you. Oh!
would that time had been granted him to

rescind his last fatal act—Oh, Cecil! it is a fatal inheritance," and covering her face she wept.

"My darling Rosamond!" he said, "are you so ill?"

"I had no wish to live," she answered, "but now . . . . "

Cecil took her slight, almost transparently white hand.

"Do you really forgive me?" she said.

"Dearest cousin, I have nothing to forgive—you have much. I know well how cruel and mean I was—ungenerous—unmanly—I see it all now. But since you are such a sweet forgiving cousin, we may yet be friends, may we not?"

"Oh, yes!" said Rosamond, "we may —we are."

At this moment Mrs. Benson entered with a tray, bringing Rosamond's luncheon.

"My dear young lady," she said, "you know you must not talk and tire yourself. Mr. Cecil, I must tell you, Miss Rosamond has been dangerously ill. The doctors almost gave her up—she is in a very precarious state now."

"You are quite mistaken," said Rosamond, with a brilliant flush and smile, " I am much better, I am almost well, for I am almost happy; I am very hungry too, you must bring me some more luncheon, and some for Mr. Cecil, unless you would rather have it in the dining-room?"

Of course Cecil preferred to have it with her. After luncheon the poor girl, fell asleep holding her cousin's hand. So still, so motionless she lay, that he could almost have fancied it was death, only there was a pale pink on her delicate cheek; her long sweeping lashes, her fine forehead, the inexpressibly sweet and placid expression of her soft features touched him deeply. In about a quarter of an hour she started up.

"I was nearly asleep, I believe," she said innocently. Cecil laughed.

"Shall we go into the garden?" she asked, "it looks fine."

She went to the window, but suddenly drew back.

"There is Stephen!" she exclaimed in a tone of disappointment.

Cecil who had followed her saw Stephen Granville, Orlando Henshawe, and old Mr. Henshawe walking up the avenue together.

"I am sorry to leave you so suddenly, dear Rosamond, but I must go," said Cecil.

"But," Rosamond inquired, " the jewels, your valuables?"

"I can write to you; I meant to leave them here, if you will kindly allow me. I only thought of taking a few to sell at present, some I have no affection for, and keep the others in reserve."

"There is a very ugly and costly gold cup and platter that Mrs. Benson says was given you when you were a child," Rosamond suggested.

"If that were disposed of, it would be

enough," said Cecil; "but I am sure you must wish to see your brother. I will not detain you. I know not how to thank you for all your undeserved goodness."

"What a hurry you are in !" said Rosamond. "How do you go ?"

"I shall walk to the station," he replied.

"Dear me !" said his cousin ; "I could walk as far as that with you."

"No, dear, it would be too much for you. Besides, I shall walk on to the farther station. I shall not get in at Deerham. There is an agricultural meeting or flower-show in the neighbourhood, and the little station is crowded. I shall enjoy the walk to Carpendon."

"Then you know the shortest way is through the shrubbery, past my old tower. Here is the key of the shrubbery gates. I always keep them locked to avoid intruders. I will send your bag to Deerham."

"Thank you. Good-bye, dearest, kindest Rosamond !"

"Good-bye, Cecil. You will come and see me again—you must, about the things left here."

"Yes, I will," said Cecil.

"Go out by the side door, and you will not have the bore of meeting any of them," she said.

He took her hand, kissed it, and left the room.

Just as he was gone there was a tap at the door. Rosamond ran and opened it, thinking it might be her cousin. It was only Sarah Benson.

"If you please, Ma'am, Mr. Henshawe, the lawyer, wishes to see you directly."

"I will come down," she answered.

In two minutes there was another tap.

"Well, what is it?" asked Rosamond, a little impatiently.

"If you please, Ma'am, Mr. Henshawe says he must speak to you immediately."

And to her surprise, she saw through the

open door Mr. Henshawe himself standing in the passage.

"I beg your pardon, Miss Granville, for intruding, but I am in some haste."

He entered the room, and looked round.

"I thought your cousin, Mr. Cecil Conway, was here."

"He is gone," said Rosamond.

"Gone!" exclaimed Mr. Henshawe, in surprise.

"Yes," Rosamond answered. "I am sorry he did not see you, but he was in a great hurry to go."

As she spoke, her brother came in, followed by Orlando Henshawe.

"Well, Miss Rosamond, you are in no hurry to see me, anyhow."

Rosamond gave him her hand and cheek rather coolly, and threw a glance of surprise at young Henshawe.

"I am sorry to disturb you," said Mr. Henshawe the elder, "but we are come on business. If you will kindly accompany me to the next room, and deliver to me your late uncle's will, we will remain in the adjoining room, according to Mr. Nicholas Conway's especial directions, and draw up the copies. Probably Mr. Cecil Conway, who I am sorry and much surprised to find is gone, may desire to have a copy also."

"I shall be very glad to have it done," said Rosamond.

Old Mr. Henshawe—who had been summoned in great haste—fixed, with some suspicion, his penetrating eyes steadily on her face as she spoke. He was satisfied; it was ingenuous as a child's.

"No doubt—no doubt, Miss Granville, it will free you from a heavy responsibility; it was a peculiarity of my friend's, Mr. Nicholas Conway, to lay it upon you, and I much regret having been unable to relieve you of it sooner."

He and Rosamond proceeded into the inner room, and she, detaching her silver key for the second time that day, gave it to Mr. Henshawe, while his son and Stephen stood expectant in the open doorway between the two rooms. Mr. Henshawe very deliberately unlocked the ancient carved cabinet, a quaint old piece of furniture, and opened it, as well as the drawer.

"By Heavens!" he exclaimed, "the will is gone!"

The two young men stepped eagerly forward. Rosamond turned deathly pale.

"Gone!" she faintly articulated, "impossible!"

Then she remembered how easily Cecil might have moved and replaced the papers in the wrong drawer by mistake. "I dare say it is in one of the other drawers," she said, half angrily at so unnecessary an alarm.

Every drawer was opened; no, too surely it was gone; each little recess and corner of the old cabinet was searched. Beneath it—behind it—around, it was nowhere to be seen. Mr. Henshawe turned to Rosamond and looked gravely in her face.

"Miss Granville," he said, "do you know where it is?"

"No," said Rosamond in the unmistakeable voice of truth. "I know nothing of it."

"You have given it to no one? You could say on your oath you know nothing of it?"

"I know nothing of it," she repeated.

"That scoundrel Cecil Conway has stolen it!" cried Stephen Granville.

"Sir, you forget yourself," said Mr. Henshawe sternly. "You do not know, perhaps, that you are accusing a person who may be innocent of a heavy crime."

"He has done it I will swear," persisted Granville, "Orlando, say what was your reason for hurrying your father up here and what you saw."

"I saw Cecil Conway with the key of

the cabinet in his hand, he had brought
from it a packet of letters. I saw him
return that key to Miss Granville."

" Is this true ?" asked the lawyer.

" Yes," Rosamond answered.

" And I myself," said Mr. Henshawe,
" saw the will lying there safe in that drawer
less than a fortnight ago. You know that
it was, Miss Granville."

" Yes," said Rosamond, scarcely able to
move her trembling lips.

" Has any other person had the key in
his possession besides Mr. Cecil Conway ?"

" Not that I know of," replied Rosamond.

" Where is Mr. Cecil Conway ?" asked
young Henshawe.

" He is gone," said Rosamond.

" Yes," observed the lawyer, " you told
me, Miss Granville, that he went away in a
great hurry."

"He must be detained!" cried Orlando Henshawe, eagerly.

"We must catch him!" Stephen said, fiercely.

"You cannot without a warrant," said Mr. Henshawe.

"Then," said his son, "Stephen and I will drive over in the dog-cart to Mr. Maltby—it will not take half-an-hour, and you, Sir, had better go to Deerham to the station and stop him. We shall not be long after you."

"It is an unjustifiable, a shameful suspicion!" exclaimed Rosamond; "it shall not be done. He is the least likely of you all to commit such an act."

"My dear Miss Granville, you will not mend matters by interfering. I regret to say that appearances are against him; but I promise that no injustice shall be done. I have a regard for the young man myself, and should deeply mourn if an unreflecting impulse had led him to commit such a crime. But I will not believe it. Probably it may still be found in some unlooked-for manner."

In the meantime, Stephen Granville and Orlando Henshawe had hurried to the stables, eager as birds of prey over a fallen victim.

"We shall have him," said the lawyer's clerk; "he can't escape us."

Granville laughed exultantly.

"My time is come now, with a vengeance. So good as this I had never hoped for!"

"You really believe he has done it?"

"Believe! I am certain he has. I only wish he could swing for it!" said Granville, savagely.

"I'm afraid those days are past, but it will be heavy enough."

So the two vultures flapped their loathsome wings over their prey.

Rosamond was now left alone. She watched the dog-cart through the gates, and saw old Mr. Henshawe slowly and reluctantly taking his way towards Deerham. Then she flew down to old Benson, and drew him out by the side door, slipping unseen with him by a small entrance into one of the stables.

"Benson," she said, "Mr. Cecil is in danger. Put my small saddle on the little black galloway, but for your life let no one see you. Bring it here."

"I will," said Benson, who knew that something wrong had happened, without guessing what.

"Now," she said, when it was ready, "listen to me, Benson. I will tie the pony to the old oak up at the farther end of the shrubbery. The old oak that was struck by lightning down by the side of the paling some way from the path—you know?"

"Yes, Miss."

"Well, when it is dark, fetch him home, but let no one see you; if you do, all is lost. If anyone is about let him loose in the paddock, and put the saddle· in the saddle-room that nothing may be suspected."

" That I will, Miss, you may trust to me. I'll think of everything."

" Thank you, kind Benson," she said, springing into the saddle.

" But let me get you a shawl, a cloak ; you are ill," said he, " it is getting chill, it is dusk."

" No, not for the world—not for a moment."

And she turned the pony on to the winding turf walk and galloped off at full speed.

She never paused until beyond the tower she came up to the gate that opened into a lonely lane. There she saw Cecil, who had loitered slowly on when once beyond the immediate neighbourhood of the house, knowing he should be early for the Carpendon train. She sprang down by his side.

"Cecil," she said, low but quietly, "you are in danger; come back with me to the tower, they are seeking you, they will take you prisoner."

"In danger! prisoner!" repeated Cecil, in amazement.

"Yes, there is no time to explain now. The will is gone—no one knows how; even Mr. Henshawe, who is your friend, says appearances are against you; they are gone to the station to arrest you."

"Do you think," said Cecil, "I would hide myself as if I were a culprit? it would be almost an admission of guilt."

"No it would not," urged Rosamond, vehemently. "Why should you submit to an undeserved indignity? and am I to have lured you here to set the blood-hounds on your track? In mercy to me—in mercy to poor Blanche, consent to keep out of the way for a time. This horrible, accursed

will may be found in a few days, why should
we all endure the agony of seeing you
dragged to prison ?   Think of Blanche."

" It would be a useless attempt, even if
I did endeavour to escape," said Cecil.

" No, you would be safe at the tower, in
the upper room, no one knows of it but
myself," Rosamond rejoined, " they will
hunt all over England before they seek you
there.   At least for a day or two, until we
have time to reflect how to act, return with
me there.   I beseech—I implore you—if
you will not—here will I die on this cold
ground."

Cecil looked at her, she had only her
usual indoor costume on ; she was fearfully
pale, with a stamp, it seemed to him, almost
of death on her face.

" I will return as you desire it, dear
Rosamond," he said, " you may be right,
although my feeling is that I would rather
face my enemies than fly them—truth is on
my side."

"Oh! may Heaven reward you for yielding your own wish to mine!" exclaimed Rosamond, passionately; "remember you can at any time come forward and confront them if there be a chance of success, if not, why should you deliver yourself up to them, and give your own hands to be bound?"

She caught the pony's bridle and flew down the wood side with it a short distance; within the paling, along a hollow or empty ditch that skirted it, she unbuckled the bridle, fastened the pony securely to a branch of the oak she had described to Benson, and having made all safe, ran back to Cecil. "Benson will take the pony back when it gets dark," she said, as she took Cecil's arm.

"Walk quick—quicker, dear Cecil," she urged.

"It will kill you," he said.

"No it will cure me," she answered, "if you escape, this day will restore me to life. I feel an energy I never knew before. I will not speak now, it retards us. I will come to you and explain all later."

They soon reached the entrance to the tower; as soon as they were within the circular room, to the surprise of Cecil, she slipped aside a square panel in the old wainscoting.

" When you get through that hole," she said, " it is easy."

He found that it led to a narrow, steep stone staircase which wound round within the tower, in total darkness. Some of the steps were broken away, but Rosamond, accustomed to the place, and as agile as a little squirrel, hurried on in front of him, and he followed. It conducted them to a pretty little apartment, with a small square of carpet on its stone flooring, and around were cushions of various sizes to repose on. The deep window-sills to the narrow slits, the only apertures in the room, were covered with scarlet cloth and performed

the office of tables. From these narrow
openings the view was beautiful, both towards the forest and mountains, and also
on the opposite side towards the open
country.

"What a pretty little hermit's cell!"
Cecil exclaimed.

"No one knows of it but me," answered
Rosamond, "some strange fancy made it
pleasant to me to keep it altogether secret
from everyone. I will bring what you
may want when it is quite safe. I dare
not stay a moment now."

Cecil took her hand and kissed it gratefully.

"To you, Rosamond, I am a very
willing prisoner."

Rosamond blushed, giving him one
gentle glance, then she ran down her
dangerous staircase, which from habit was
as easy to her as the broad flights of steps
in Crown-Harden mansion, and running
and walking by turns reached again the

side-door she had shortly before left.

It was late, when generally all was closed for the night, still had she been obliged to ring for admittance it would not have caused any surprise; for her ways of going on, as the servants declared, were so very uncommon. She often rambled about late, to the horror of poor Sarah Benson, who, had she lived in the middle ages, would have no doubt believed that her young mistress, from her strange wild ways, must have had dealings with the spirits.

But Benson had taken good care that she should meet with no inconvenience. He had allowed the doors to be locked, and then quietly, unknown to anyone, had again unfastened the side-door where his young mistress would re-enter the house.

Rosamond silently and unperceived returned to her sofa in the library, while no person except Benson dreamt that she had ever left it. She had but just composed herself, when there was a tap at the door, and the elder Mr. Henshawe entered the room.

CHAPTER XXI.

IF you are well enough, my dear Miss Granville, I wished to have a little conversation with you," said Mr. Henshawe.

" I am quite ready to attend to you," she answered.

" You are a young lady of so much sense and discernment," he began, " that I thought it might be acceptable to you, as well as a satisfaction to me, to place before you this unfortunate case exactly as it stands, at least as far as, according to my poor ability, I can do so."

" Indeed, Mr. Henshawe," she replied,

"you have guessed my wish. I much desire to understand it clearly, and do not fear to put all before me in the worst light for my dear cousin, that I may judge how great the danger is. As to his innocence, you may rest assured I am as confident of it as of my own."

"I will disguise nothing from you, and you may depend on my always acting with perfect openness towards you. I need not tell you how deeply painful to me it will be if I have to take proceedings against any of the family, more especially that fine young man, Mr. Cecil Conway, but I am bound to perform my duty. I have seen Sir Charles Townsend, my colleague in the management of your affairs, and he agrees with me that this course is inevitable."

"What course?" asked Rosamond hastily.

"That we must take measures against Mr. Cecil Conway."

"He has nothing to do with it," said Rosamond.

"If so, my dear young lady, nothing will be so advantageous to him as a most thorough investigation of every circumstance that can be elicited. As matters now stand, I am bound to say that he lies under the very strongest suspicion. I am compelled unwillingly to acknowledge that even if it were possible to quash the whole business entirely—which it is not—his honour and good name would be forfeited."

"It will be well," said Rosamond, "if the truth can be established, but this is not always the case in law proceedings."

"We can but do our best to exert all the prudence and discrimination possible, as far as in us lies," Mr. Henshawe answered. "Will you inform me whether you think it possible that anyone can have obtained possession of your key since I saw the documents a fortnight back?"

"I think not," Rosamond replied.

",There your statement agrees with that of your lady's-maid, Sarah Benson, who told me that at that time she sewed the end of the chain whereby it is attached to the waist of your dress, and also that you have worn the same dress every day since without any change."

" I believe so," said Rosamond.

" She also mentioned that at night your dress hangs in a wardrobe within your bed-room."

" Yes," Rosamond answered.

" And that the key being attached to the chain by a small padlock, the key of which is fastened to your watch-chain, no one could possibly obtain possession of the key unknown to you."

"I suppose not," she said ; "but perhaps some other key might open the cabinet."

" Excuse me," the lawyer continued, " your key is of a most singular and un- usual form. I have never seen any other of that description; the wards are in the form of a Latin cross."

" Could not an impression be taken and another such key be made from it ?" Rosamond inquired.

"A most pertinent suggestion," remarked the old lawyer, " but we have not overlooked such a possibility, though, it is so remote as to amount to almost an impossibility. No one at Deerham or in the neighbourhood could manufacture a key like this; there are other reasons too that make it appear impossible · —but that question will of course be thoroughly sifted. You must also reflect on the extreme difficulty of obtaining access to the cabinet for such a purpose, the doors being always locked at night, and usually in the day-time. I must not omit another circumstance that proves clearly that it was not the work of a common thief. As you know, in a small compartment of the very drawer where the wills were deposited, is a collection of valuable unset stones—diamonds, rubies, &c., cut, but loose, as well as some gold coins—all of which are left untouched, undisturbed. The will, and that alone, was the object of the robbery. Who has any interest whatever in the will, except your brother, yourself, and Mr. Cecil and Miss Conway? Your brother, excuse my even naming him in connection with such a transaction, has been absent two months, and only returned to-day."

Rosamond hesitated, she was unwilling to pain the worthy man—yet there was another, the only one she thought likely to be suspected in this terrible uncertainty.

" And Mr. Orlando Henshawe?" . . . .

His father coloured deeply. " Of course my son has no right to be exempt any more than another person, if a shade of suspicion could attach to him; but he has been abroad part of the time, and as you well know, Miss Granville, he has received from yourself an injunction never to trespass on your privacy—never to approach the library or study uncalled, nor has he done so. He could scarcely, even in your absence, enter the study unperceived. He would have to pass the housekeeper's room, where Mrs Benson always sits, and also upstairs the room where your maid, Sarah Benson, is constantly at work, and who for some reason or other seems to keep a somewhat close watch upon him."

Rosamond knew this to be the case, not only because they were conscious of her antipathy to him, but from an aversion and suspicion they themselves entertained of the gentleman. She could not help confessing to herself that it seemed—yes —it was impossible he could ever have had the opportunity of examining, or taking impressions from the lock of the cabinet. There was a pause, then almost

ashamed of the absurdity of the suggestion, she murmured, "Richard Conway."

"My dear young lady," said the lawyer,
smiling, "I fear we can have no recourse
to him. What possible reason could he
have for so acting? even had it been possible for him more than for another.
Can you fancy that excellent gentleman
stealthily procuring an imitation of your
key? A man so scrupulous and modest
that he scarcely dares take his own hat off
the hall-table? · I will frankly tell you
that he did once express a slight degree of
regret that your cousins had not been
better treated, and observed that the will
he concluded must indubitably stand good.
Whereupon I told him that so many witnesses had heard the reading of it, and
could vouch for the contents, that there
could be no dispute, even though the will
itself were to disappear."

"Then," said Rosamond, where is the

necessity for all this trouble and misery?
why not leave it so?"

"Do you not see that every person in
the house, and many others, know of its
abstraction?" said Mr. Henshawe, "a
crime is publicly known to have been committed; though I cannot instruct you in
law details sufficiently for you to understand them, you can comprehend that
although the disposal of the property may
be altered—though no room may be left for
dispute—yet the value of it and the powers
over it are most considerably diminished,
most seriously impaired. Why, Madam,
what a flaw in the title to the estate."

And the professional feelings of the
lawyer caused him to stand more aghast
than even when his son was by implication
brought under suspicion.

"Mr. Cecil Conway was, perhaps, the
only person ignorant of this fact—namely,
that the abstraction of the will would not
invalidate your rights and claims."

"Oh ! that is too far-fetched !" exclaimed Rosamond.

"I believe you wish to be informed of every plea that can be brought against your cousin," said Mr. Henshawe. "Unhappily there are many more. His hasty flight has not a favourable appearance."

"That I could explain," said Rosamond. The lawyer bowed.

"His purpose, at least, his ostensible purpose in coming was to take possession and remove all the jewels and valuables that you declare belong to him, by gift or otherwise. He has not touched one, in his hasty flight he has abandoned them all."

"He agreed to leave them here with me for safety sake, and only to have one article sold, the gold cup and platter," explained Rosamond.

"Surely such a decision might have been expressed by letter. Have you any objection to inform me where he now is living ?"

" I do not know," Rosamond answered.

" You do not know! how very strange! He concealed from you his present dwelling place ?"

" I never asked it," she replied ; she did not explain that her quick perceptions had told her that he did not wish her to inquire.

" I will now inform you," continued Mr. Henshawe, " what steps have been taken. The warrant is, of course, procured. Nothing could be heard of Mr. Cecil Conway at the station, but the place was so unusually crowded by persons returning from the Agricultural Exhibition, that we are not surprised at that circumstance. My son has gone up to town, but will probably return here to-morrow. Mr. Stephen Granville, who seems determined to leave no chances open, has thought proper to go to —— and will visit other places on the sea-coast, thinking it probable he may seek to embark for the Continent. I am returning home for to-day, though I may have to trench on your hospitality later. I shall to-morrow morning be with Sir Charles Townsend, but if you wish to see me I am at your service, and a message either to Sir Charles Townsend's, or at my office, will be attended to at once."

"Thank you," said Rosamond, concealing, with the utmost caution, the relief it gave her to know that her enemies were distant at present, at least.

"Shall you come up here later in the afternoon?" she inquired.

"If I receive any intelligence that can be of interest to you, you may be sure that I shall—not otherwise."

"Thank you," repeated Rosamond; "but will not you sleep here to-night?"

To her inexpressible comfort the offer she had felt constrained to make was declined, and a deep sigh of thankfulness escaped her when she heard the lawyer's old-fashioned equipage come to the door and drive off.

As soon as he was gone, Mrs. Benson appeared.

"Oh! thank heaven, Miss Rosamond, dear, we have got shet of 'em all at last! What! do they want to make out that our young Master Cecil stole the will? A set of villains!"

"They do, but they never will," Rosamond answered.

"Not if there's justice in the land, but by what I've seen there is not much. Oh, if Mr. Cecil were but rich as he ought to be, they'd never dare so to abuse him. What will you have for supper, Miss Rosamond?"

"I feel quite exhausted," she answered, "do bring me something substantial, and wine; I must have a double share to-night."

"Glad of it, my dear, you never do take enough. No wonder you feel faint and empty. I do, I know."

A very amply supplied tray was brought up.

" Let the servants go to bed," said Rosamond, " I dare say they are tired. I cannot just yet; I feel too excited to sleep, I shall try to read a little. Good night."

" Good night, my dear young lady, but Sarah had better wait to undress you."

" No, it would only worry me to think I was keeping her up."

" You're so thoughtful, and always was, Miss Rosamond," said the good woman.

Rosamond sat listening, hearing the distant doors shut one after another; then followed that deep stillness there is in a house when all have retired to rest. She fancied that the gentle sighing of the April breeze among the trees sounded like the whispers of spirits. It was a dark, but not a black night.

Rosamond collected from the tray what she thought Cecil would like, and what she could carry, and went out, her heart beating very fast. She was too imaginative to possess the cool courage of Blanche, but she was as firm in her resolves when once taken.

Poor old Turk gave one suppressed, mournful howl as she passed near his kennel, and the sound sent all the blood rushing from her heart. It seemed to have a melancholy foreboding tone. Under the trees it was very dark, but she knew the way too well to feel any hesitation, only it appeared much longer than at other times; and on turning the corner where she came first in sight of the tower, she started—it stood so tall, so massive, so black against the dim sky.

She entered, and soon found her way up-stairs, and then for the first time a sudden timidity and confusion oppressed her, and she scarcely dared take the last step into the apartment.

Cecil came forward.

"Rosamond," he said gently, and held his hand to help her in.

"I have brought you a little supper," she said, in her old shy voice.

"Oh, thank you," he answered, "how kind you are, sit down and rest; these cushions in the corner are very comfortable."

"Only for a few minutes," she said. "I hear that Mr. Villeroy is returned from his tour, and is alone at Deerham Park; do you think that he could be of any use to us? I am sure he would."

"What, to please you, Rosamond? Blanche thinks he likes you very much," said Cecil.

The colour rushed to her face, dark as it was.

"He—he was always very kind to me," she answered a little embarrassed.

"I do not see what he could do," Cecil observed a little pettishly.

"I was thinking," said Rosamond, "Blanche may be very uneasy; you say she does not wish it to be known where she is. I think we must not venture to write to her, lest in any way the letter should be intercepted. If this wretched mystery is not cleared up at once, I thought Mr. Villeroy might go where she is, and have some communication with Blanche."

"You think of everything, Rosamond. Yes, it might be so, unless I went myself."

"Oh, not yet—wait a little," she implored. "Perhaps the will may yet come to light. Its disappearance seems inexplicable."

"I quite see," said Cecil, "that even an unprejudiced person might, under the circumstances, suspect me; but, Rosamond, I am not guilty. Do you believe me?"

"Believe you!" she repeated, and added earnestly: "I could scarcely believe you guilty if you told me you were so."

"Generous girl!" exclaimed Cecil. "Oh, Rosamond, you do indeed heap burning coals on my head. If I were condemned,

I believe it would be penal servitude for life. What would become of Blanche ?"

"Do not speak of it," she cried. "It will never be. I will tell you, Cecil, if affairs look threatening, what you might do, if it should come to the worst—dress as a girl. I could bring you the things. You would make a beautiful girl."

Cecil laughed.

"Rather an awkward one," he remarked.

"Leave here before dawn, walk across the hills to Baltyre—that is out of our beat —get into the train on the South-Western line, and at Lymington, or some quiet place, go on board a steamboat, or Mr. Villeroy might take you off in his yacht. There are only two people I dread for you —my cruel brother and that horrible Mr. Orlando Henshawe; but I can always know their movements through Mr. Henshawe, and of course you would take an opposite direction from theirs. Blanche could rejoin you abroad after a time."

" I do not think I could skulk away like a thief," said Cecil; " but we have time before us, and can consider what is best, thanks to your generous assistance. As you say, the mystery may be cleared up shortly. If so, I shall be thankful to escape the dishonour, the ignominy . . . . And Blanche, who is so proud, will not suffer the agony of . . . . " He could not bring out the words, but held his hands before his face, and with difficulty repressed a sob. " We have been thoughtless and unfeeling, but now we are made to feel."

" Oh, Cecil, forbear," said Rosamond, weeping. " We must think of nothing now but hope; it is above all courage we need. Do not even glance on the dark side."

" My dear little cousin must not stay here too long. You will be ill; you exert yourself too much," he said.

" No, no. I have not been so strong for

months," she replied. "But perhaps I had better go. Good night."

"Good night," said Cecil. He held her two hands in his a moment, then passed his arm round her waist, and pressed her one short moment to his heart. He could not help it; but he drew back the next.

"Forgive me!" he said, but she was gone. A chill fell over him as he lost sight of her. The warmth, sunshine, and music of life were withdrawn with her; a vault-like coldness enshrouded him. How could he ever dream of happiness again? Joy and hope were shut out. The future stood threatening against him, stern, im- moveable as a material barrier; like a wall of black rock bounding his horizon, against which the dearest hopes of his soul, like waves, must dash themselves in vain, to be beaten back in froth and foam. Yes, he must cease to struggle, and learn to re- sign. For youth and passion, how hard a task!

He was alone and in darkness, with none near to pity or to mock. He knelt low, and the tears rained down fast on the stone pavement, unbidden, but unchecked.

CHAPTER XXII.

WHILE this was passing, Mr. Orlando Henshawe was paying a visit to Mr. Smith in Pall Mall. There he learnt all that Mr. Smith knew, that Mr. and Miss Conway had taken apartments at Mrs. Garratt's in Berkley Street.

He at once repaired thither and knocked. The servant girl ran to the door, but shrank back at the aspect of Mr. Orlando Henshawe. Though he was called young Mr. Henshawe, he was thirty at least, and not merely a very plain man, but endowed with a most repulsive countenance when not in some measure disguised by an assumed smile. His thin, lanky, pale hair looked moist and unhealthy; his cat-like eyes, pointed chin, and unusual width from ear to ear gave him an expression of dangerous cunning; but now, added to all, there was a fierce, sharp, hungry keenness about his sallow face that inspired dread as well as disgust.

He thirsted for revenge, a passion that may sound poetical in a Red Indian or Corsican bandit, but that in the real man is hideous; he pined for the ruin—if it were possible the blood—of the man he hated, and the evil spirit within him shone out from his eyes.

"Is Miss Conway at home?" he asked.

"Miss Conway has left," the girl said, half closing the door against him, while he set his foot to push it back.

"I must speak to Mrs. Garratt, I have important business with Mr. Conway. Where is he?"

"I don't know, Sir."

"What train did he go by?"

" By the South-Western," she unad-
visedly answered.

He came into the hall with a smile that
drew down the corners of his mouth.

" Mr. Conway has gone to a friend, I
suppose," he observed.

" I think to some country place, Sir, I
don't know, unless it was an abbey. I
will send Mrs. Garratt, Sir."

He walked into the landlady's little
back-room at the end of the passage, and
by and bye Mrs. Garratt made her appearance, after putting on a clean cap.
Conscious in some degree of something
uninviting in the expression of his countenance, Orlando Henshawe took the precaution of turning his back to the small
window with its crotchet work half-blind.

" I have business of importance with
Mr. Cecil Conway, and it is necessary to
lose no time. I dare say," he continued
in his most oily tones, " you, my dear lady,
can assist me to find him."

" I think not, Sir," said Mrs. Garratt drily, warned by some instinct, the same that makes us turn with repulsion from the scent of certain deadly poisons.

" Do not you forward letters to them ?" he inquired, with a little escape of fierceness.

" They don't seem to have many friends, Sir," she answered evasively.

" Then you do not choose to tell me where they are," he said, perceiving that cajolery would be utterly useless.

" I am sure, Sir, I would serve them willingly if I could; Mr. Conway was very pleasant-spoken and quite the gentleman —a perfect gentleman," she repeated with a certain intonation that said, " I doubt whether you are."

Henshawe banged the door open violently with an oath, and marched out into the street without deigning to shut it behind him.

" Lord, Ma'am," said the maid, coming

forward and shutting it cautiously, " what a dreadful man !"

" You told him nothing, I hope," said Mrs. Garratt.

"Oh dear, no, Ma'am," said the maid; but she was wrong, she had told him enough.

He waited till he got back to his little room in Red Lion Square, and then sat down to reflect.

" The South-Western line, the country, an abbéy." Not much to go upon, but it was enough for him. He sprang up, clapping his hands together emphatically. " I have it," he said, " Villeroy's uncle— Holland Abbey."

Without delay he went off by the train, stopping at the neighbouring town where Blanche and Cecil had remained until their cottage was ready.

He soon made acquaintance with the landlord of the small inn, sported his money freely, and speedily learnt all that the man was able to tell him. He had imagined in the first instance that they were guests of Sir Philip Holland, and was astonished to find that they were, instead, humble dependants. His haughty enemy a gamekeeper, and soon to be a felon! He laughed exultingly, and rubbed his large hands together.

"So," he said sneeringly, "they call themselves Crawford, do they? Charles Crawford—and the girl?"

"Well," replied the landlord, "I think it was Bertha; some grand name with a B."

"Exactly!" laughed Orlando Henshawe; "C. C. and B. C.; their right initials, that's all. My good man, their name is Crawford just as much as yours is."

"Sure!" exclaimed the landlord, "but is there anything against them?"

"Against them? I should rather think so," said Henshawe; "but is the young man come back?"

"Well, I should say he is," replied the

landlord, who was not anxious to lose so good a customer, and who had heard that Crawford was to return in three days. " Our squire, Sir Philip Holland, only gave him three days, and he's not a gentleman to be trifled with."

It was on that evening that Orlando Henshawe stole round the cottage, hoping to catch sight of Cecil; till late at night he prowled wolf-like around, not returning to his inn till near morning.

About ten o'clock he called at Holland Abbey, sent in his card to Sir Philip, begging a few minutes' audience on important business, and desiring the servant to mention that he was an acquaintance of Mr. Stephen Granville, of Crown-Harden House, and that his profession was the law—little guessing that Sir Philip hated Stephen Granville and abhorred lawyers.

" Show the animal in," was Sir Philip's polite invitation.

On Mr. Orlando Henshawe's entrance,

Sir Philip stared at him from head to foot. His appearance spoke no better on his behalf than it did in Berkley Street; he began fumbling eagerly in his pocket-book, greatly offended at his mode of reception, with an air half-defying, half-mean.

"I doubt, Sir Philip, when you learn the favour I . . . ."

"If you come here with begging letters," said Sir Philip, "you're losing your time; I never give."

Mr. Henshawe felt sharply aggrieved, but smiled.

"Not very likely, Sir Philip. The favour I spoke of when you interrupted me was not one I desired to ask, but rather to grant."

There was something in the tone of the last words, pompous, yet threatening, that in a person so greatly his inferior, appeared to Sir Philip equally ridiculous and insolent.

"What, a threatening letter by word of mouth!" he scoffed.

"No, Sir," was the reply, as the insulted visitor drew himself up with an assumption of dignity that made Sir Philip laugh. "You have a person of the name of Conway in your employment, I believe?"

"Conway? No, I haven't," said Sir Philip.

"I beg your pardon, Crawford he calls himself; but that is not his real name."

"Indeed!" said Sir Philip, coldly.

"The hand of justice is over him."

"Are you justice, pray?" inquired Sir Philip.

"Permit me to demand from you an explicit answer. Has he returned to his duties here?"

"You had better find out!" rejoined Sir Philip, his growing anger beginning to boil over.

"I tell you, Sir, there is reason to believe that the person you vainly endeavour to

screen has committed a crime. I can produce——"

"Be off!" shouted Sir Philip, in extreme
wrath, and determined to hear no more,
lest he should be obliged to pay attention
to the man's business, having from the first
moment conceived the most violent contempt and aversion for him. "Be off, and
do not loiter about my premises, or it may
be worse for you. I warn you!"

And he rang his bell in a rage.

"And I warn *you*," persisted Henshawe,
"I can produce the warrant."

But as he looked round Sir Philip Holland was gone, and a man-servant entering
politely opened the door for him and bowed
him out, white with suppressed fury. Not,
however, to go farther than his inn at the
town, for he thought it probable that Cecil
would rejoin his sister, and both go abroad
together; or that in any case he would be
certain to communicate with her, and
thus he could make use of Blanche as

a decoy-bird to capture her brother.

As he knew nothing of Stephen Granville's encounter with Conway at this place, he imagined that both Cecil and Blanche would feel themselves secure and unknown near Holland Abbey; and that in all probability it would be the most likely spot for Cecil to visit before leaving England.

His hatred was as virulent as young Granville's. It was sharpened by jealousy, for he had not even now abandoned his pretensions to the hand of Rosamond Granville. When she had been living on the charity of her uncle, treated with even less respect than poor relations generally meet with, he had in his self-conceit imagined that his marrying her would be a great rise in life for the neglected orphan.

He saw her in her faded cotton gowns and shabby merinos, scolded by her uncle, even in his presence, slighted and disregarded by all; and her pale, serious countenance, and silent, undemonstrative manners he mistook for humility, little guessing that the shy girl was as proud as her gay and favoured young cousin.

He really believed that he would be doing a noble and generous action by marrying her, and raising her to independence and affluence, yet at the same time his ambition would be gratified. It would ally him not only with the Conways, who were considered to be among the principal people in the neighbourhood, but also with the highly connected Granvilles; and such a connection, although worthless when combined with poverty, would be both advantageous and honourable to a man who was rich, as he expected to be at his father's death. He had also discrimination enough to see that she was lady-like, and later, when set off by handsome and becoming dress, her elegance and high-bred air excited his admiration; and such love as he was capa-

ble of feeling, not pure, but violent, inflamed his fancy.

Her coldness and disdain enraged,
without discouraging him; he was not
conscious of his own utter unworthiness
and demerits, but supposing himself to be
far more clever than the rest of the world,
he saw no reason why he should not eventu-
ally succeed; therefore he ascribed his ill-
fortune solely to a stupid preference for
another, and that other could be only
Cecil Conway.

In secret, he half hated her for her
blindness in preferring a good-looking
fool, as he considered Cecil, to a man so
superior as himself, and ridiculed her for
what he imagined was a silly infatuation
for a handsome coxcomb who regarded
her with utter indifference. Sometimes he
felt as if he could almost strangle her for
her provoking and senseless affection for
the man he abhorred; at others, he would
have sacrificed much to win one of her

quiet smiles; but his rancour against Cecil never varied, never diminished. Even when at times a panic seized him, lest Villeroy should after all be the happy man, he still cherished an unabated malignity against both the brother and sister. Their easy, careless, slighting manner, and air of unintentional superiority, evidently showing that in their eyes he was of no account whatever—a mere lawyer's clerk—enraged him far more than studied rudeness would have done.

There was another sore place rankling in his evil heart. Why did not his father take him into partnership? Why degrade him, when he was a man of the mature age of thirty, by still keeping him as only a kind of upper clerk? Poor Mr. Henshawe would gladly have given him the share he coveted; but he saw with grief and regret the bad and dangerous character of his only son. He believed that the less power he gave him, the less mischief he would do, and intended to re-sign his business altogether as soon as his tardy arrangements should be com-pleted with a successor.

END OF THE SECOND VOLUME.

London: Printed by A. Schulze, 13, Poland Street.

www.ingramcontent.com/pod-product-compliance
Lightning Source LLC
Chambersburg PA
CBHW060556030726
47498CB00005B/1421